'Absolutely top-notch. So many twists it makes me dizzy thinking about it'

Jo Jakeman, author of *Safe House*

'Dark and twisted, but with sunshine and nostalgia to transport you'

SJI Holliday, author of *Violet*

'Wow, wow, wow. Katerina Diamond has not disappointed!' ***** Reader Review

'A brilliant whodunnit story with an incredible twist' ***** Reader Review

'So many twists and turns and an excellent ending I didn't see coming'

***** Reader Review

'I was hooked straightaway ... kept me guessing until its shocking ending'

***** Reader Review

Also by Katerina Diamond

KATERINA DIAMOND burst onto the crime scene with her debut *The Teacher*, which became a *Sunday Times* bestseller and a number one Kindle bestseller. It was longlisted for the CWA John Creasey Debut Dagger Award and the Hotel Chocolat Award for 'darkest moment'. *The Teacher* was followed by sequels *The Secret*, *The Angel*, *The Promise*, *Truth or Die* and *Woman in the Water*, all of which featured detectives Adrian Miles and Imogen Grey. *The Heatwave* is her first stand-alone thriller.

Katerina has lived in various glamorous locations such as Weston-Super-Mare, Thessaloniki, Larnaca, Exeter, Derby and Forest Gate. Katerina now resides in East Kent with her husband and children. She was born on Friday 13th.

The
Heatwave
Katerina Diamond

avon.

Published by AVON
A division of HarperCollins*Publishers* Ltd
1 London Bridge Street
London SE1 9GF

www.harpercollins.co.uk

A Paperback Original 2020

First published in Great Britain by HarperCollins*Publishers* 2020

A catalogue copy of this book is
available from the British Library.

ISBN-13: 978-0-00-836180-8

This novel is entirely a work of fiction.
The names, characters and incidents portrayed in it are
the work of the author's imagination. Any resemblance to
actual persons, living or dead, events or localities is
entirely coincidental.

Typeset in Sabon LT Std by Palimpsest Book Production Ltd,
Falkirk, Stirlingshire
Printed and bound in UK by CPI Group (UK) Ltd, Croydon CR0 4YY

MIX
Paper from
responsible sources
FSC **FSC® C007454**
www.fsc.org

This book is produced from independently certified FSC™ paper to
ensure responsible forest management.

For more information visit: www.harpercollins.co.uk/green

To my step-dad, Roger.
Thanks for taking care of my mum,
so I don't have to.

Prologue

The gears stick as the car is changed into third. From the back seat she can hear the crunching with each gear shift. Outside the dusky sky darkens with each passing moment. She looks in the footwell of the seat next to her, where there is a bag full of water bottles.

'Have one of those if you want,' the driver says, their eyes connecting in the rear-view mirror.

'Just up here, thanks,' the girl says, opening a bottle and drinking thirstily.

The car keeps going, past the road her home is on. She taps on the window. 'You can just drop me here. I can walk this last bit.'

The car keeps moving. The girl realises the driver has no intention of stopping. She tugs at the handle but the back door is locked, the mechanism snapped off. She slams her palm against the window, smacking repeatedly, hoping someone, anyone will walk past and hear.

The car speeds up and the girl starts to feel strange, a bitter taste in the back of her throat. She feels the cold water splash against her thighs as she drops the bottle, her grip too weak to hold on. She lolls in her seat, unable to stay upright. She slumps to the side, the feebleness in her hand spreading to the rest of her body. She knows she is in trouble. She struggles to stay awake, aware that once her eyes are closed, they may never open again. As her lids draw together she tries to speak, but all she hears is an unintelligible gargle.

'You're coming with me,' the driver says.

Chapter One

Now

The bed next to me is empty when I wake, my eyes still puffy from crying myself to sleep while listening to the radio for comfort. Chris never came upstairs to bed. At his work event last night I drank too much and locked myself in the toilet. Social situations make me anxious and as understanding as he is, I always push him past his limit. I had promised to behave myself this time, but as usual my nerves got the better of me and I embarrassed him again, something I seem to do more and more these days. My head is throbbing, I know I haven't slept well, the echo of my dreams still lingering. They're indiscernible, but I have the uneasy feeling that comes after a nightmare.

I wander downstairs in my pyjamas and find Chris asleep on the sofa where I left him last night, an overturned wineglass on the rug and the TV on. I reach down and feel for wetness but there is nothing. At least he finished the wine before he dropped the glass. I pull the throw on the back of the sofa over him. I wonder how long he will keep up the silent treatment this time. It's nothing less than I deserve.

'What time is it?' he mutters.

'It's still early – it's seven – the kids aren't even awake yet. Why don't you go and get in bed for a couple of hours?' I suggest, trying not to sound upset.

'I wanted to go out on the bike this morning.'

'Oh. I thought we were having a lazy weekend.'

'I've changed my mind.'

'If you're annoyed at me, will you just bloody say it? I can't stand this tension between us.' The tears start again.

'Come here.'

I get on the sofa next to him and he pulls me into an embrace. Kissing my tears away, then kissing me on the lips. He gets like this the morning after he's been drinking. His hands start to wander and I know he isn't angry with me anymore.

'Not here.'

'Come on, you already said the kids were still asleep.'

'They could wake up at any moment.'

'We'll hear them; you know they find it impossible to stay quiet.' He kisses me again and I sink into the sofa – feeling him against me like this is always nice. I am half in the moment and half listening out for any movement in the house, not wanting to traumatise our children by having them walk in on us in flagrante on the couch.

As Chris kisses down my body the words from the television start to permeate my thoughts. It's a news report about a missing girl last seen at a bus stop in a sleepy seaside town on the south coast . . . no clues as to what happened to her. I push against Chris to get him to move but he just keeps kissing me.

'What is it?' he says as he realises I'm not just offering friendly resistance.

'The news, I need to hear it.'

'Are you joking?' He gets up and sits back with a petulant sigh.

I grab the remote and rewind the report. Images of a small town in Devon, quaint and picturesque. Just what you would imagine on a postcard from the south of England, lots of pebbles and red cliffs and hanging baskets full of pansies. The reporter standing at the bus stop is telling the story of a young girl, Mandy Green, who went missing just a few days earlier. The police believe it's a possible kidnapping. The story ends with a sweeping view of the coastline, all the candy-coloured hotels along the shore. I stand.

'I have to go,' I say, knowing he will ask me questions. I don't want to answer them right now; I don't know how to. The news report is so familiar, it's almost the same as one I saw many years ago, of the girl who went missing and was never seen again. Same town. I feel sick at the thought of history repeating itself in any way. I thought I had put a stop to all of that when I left.

'Go where?'

'Devon.'

'What are you talking about?'

'I know that place, Sidmouth, it's where I grew up.'

'There? That's not what I expected. I thought you didn't want to talk about your home because it was rough. That place looks like something out of a posh period drama.'

'Not rough, just . . . not what it seems.' How do I explain to him, with his perfectly open family and no understanding of what it feels like to be trapped inside someone else's lies?

'Well, I can't take any time off right now, but after next Thursday we could all drive down. You could show us around some of your old haunts – I bet the kids would love it.'

'No. No, I don't want you to come. I need to go on my own.'

'Today? It's Saturday. We were going to take the kids to the cinema later. I don't see why this can't wait until Monday, at least.'

'I'm sorry. I really need to go. You can manage without me for once,' I say, as though he is being unreasonable to expect me to explain myself.

'This is ridiculous. You can't just keep a whole part of yourself cut off from us, we're your family. Why do you think our teenage daughter only comes to me when she has a problem? Why do you think Lloyd won't talk to us about what's going on at school? You're so closed off, Flick, you need to let us in. We're your family. It's supposed to be us against the world and it really doesn't feel that way.'

'I know, and I'm sorry. I need to go back though; I need to confront those demons or I will never be able to change. I can't help the way I am.'

'Well, you need to try, or you are going to lose those kids.'

'I wasn't always like this. Maybe finally going

home will help me work through my issues – like *you* wanted me to.' I don't leave him any room to protest. 'I'll arrange for an after-school club for Lloyd and go down tonight. It's the last couple of weeks of term anyway, it's not like they do any proper classes. Daisy will be all right with him 'til you get home from work.'

'It's that important?'

'I wouldn't ask you if it wasn't. Please, Chris, just let me do this. I promise when I get back I'll tell you everything.'

'Why now? What's this about the missing girl? Do you know her?'

I hesitate. 'No, but when I was at school a girl went missing. I was with her the night she disappeared.'

'Jesus, why didn't you tell me?'

'I find it hard to talk about the past, you know I do,' I say.

'Did the police ever find out what happened to her?'

'No. She vanished without a trace.'

There's a tiny part of me that hopes that I am wrong, a part of me that hopes there is no connection between the two disappearances. The news report has forced me to remember that summer when everything changed. I try not to think about that time and I have never spoken about it since, especially not to Chris. It's a secret I have kept locked away. But there is no hiding from it anymore.

I have to go back.

Chapter Two

Then

Jasmine's father pushed her bed so that it faced the feature wall. It was papered with a mural of a tropical beach at sunset. She would have preferred something a little simpler, more grown up, but didn't want to say anything because her parents were so pleased. Jasmine's mother Lisa helped her make the bed with brilliant white bedding and the Kantha quilt that she had coveted for years. It had been given to the Burgess family by the women from a village in Bangladesh they had visited a few years ago, and Lisa had given it to her daughter to mark her sixteenth birthday. It depicted vibrant parrots on a deep green background, with yellow stitching running all the way through the quilt.

'Doesn't this look perfect in here? I hope you look after it, Jazz. This is a one of a kind,' Lisa said.

'If you don't trust me with it then keep it,' Jasmine said, gripping the edge of the quilt, ready to hold on in case her mother changed her mind and decided to put it back in the cupboard.

'Of course I trust you,' Lisa said.

'Is that everything then?' Frank asked, tilting his head and looking at the curtain pole over the window, checking it was straight.

'Yes. Everything is brilliant, now let me get settled please,' Jasmine said impatiently, desperate for some time alone in her new room.

Her dad came over to ruffle her hair as though she were a child, and she shrugged him off instinctively.

'Fine. Call if you need us,' Lisa said as she reluctantly left the room.

Her parents went down the hall to finish their own unpacking.

The house was bigger than their old one, where Jasmine's room had been a third the size of this one, and they'd had a courtyard rather than a garden. Jasmine had the feeling she was betraying her old self by living on this road, where the snobby kids lived, so she was determined not to become like them.

Jasmine's bedroom window looked out over the overgrown garden, to where a small, painted brick, chalet-type guest house was tucked into the corner. Frank and Lisa planned to rent it out to fund their trips abroad.

She went down to the kitchen and grabbed a banana from the fruit bowl. They hadn't had a chance to do a proper shop yet. As Jasmine made her way back to her room, she heard a knock on the front door. She looked in the mirror. She wasn't properly dressed or showered, and her hair looked a little bedraggled, but no one else was coming down to answer.

She opened the door to see a man much younger than her father standing there with a holdall over his shoulder. He was looking at the ground so all she could really tell about him was that he had very dark blond hair, which was brushed back away from his face. When he peeked out from beneath his eyebrows he seemed surprised to see her and stood up straighter. His eyes slowly wandered over Jasmine and she crossed her arms across her front. She couldn't quite read the look on his face, but it was as though he was re-evaluating something.

'I'm looking for Frank and Lisa Burgess,' he said. His tone was unfriendly.

She suddenly wished she was wearing something other than shorts, and crossed one foot in front of the other in an attempt at modesty.

Jasmine turned to the stairwell and shouted, 'Dad! There's someone here for you.'

Moments later Frank appeared, peering around the corner at the top of the stairs. His face lit up when he saw their visitor and he rushed down, arm extended to shake the other man's hand.

'I'm not too early, am I? I can come back if you're busy,' the stranger said with a smile, much warmer than he had been a moment ago. He almost pushed Jasmine out of the way as he moved towards her father.

'Lisa!' Frank called up the stairs. 'Tim's here.'

Jasmine heard her mother's excited exclamation and then before she knew it, Lisa was downstairs with her arms around Tim's neck in a hug. When Lisa pulled away, Jasmine could see immediately that her mother was attracted to him; she looked flustered. As they talked about how unpleasant the blistering heat outside was, Jasmine took the time to look at their visitor. He was tall and, although she wouldn't call him good looking, he wasn't ugly; there was something interesting about his face. As he put his holdall on the floor, his shirt lifted up a little and she could see there was a tattoo across his hip, although she couldn't see what it was. She noted he had an avocado-sized patch of sweat at the small of his back but other than that you wouldn't know he had just been outside in this ungodly heat. His skin was tanned, as though he spent a lot of time outside in the sun, and he had tiny flecks of bright white paint on both his face and his muscular arms.

Lisa seemed to remember her daughter was there and turned to her. 'Jasmine, I want you to meet Tim. Tim's the man decorating the house for us; he did your bedroom.'

'Thanks,' she said, unsure what the proper response was and feeling even more uncomfortable knowing that he had been in her bedroom. That he'd put her new bed together, touched almost every surface.

Her father ushered Tim into the kitchen and her mother followed behind. For a moment she reminded Jasmine of the girls in school who would follow the boys around and hang on their every word. She suppressed the urge to roll her eyes.

Jasmine gleaned from the conversation that Tim was going to be moving into the guest house in the garden, which made her feel uneasy. She also noticed that he seemed to know her mother better than her father; Lisa had worked with him before in some capacity. None of them addressed Jasmine as they talked, as if she wasn't there. But as soon as her parents looked at each other, or were distracted, Tim threw quick glances towards Jasmine, as though he didn't want her there. When his eyes met hers, she looked away. There was something so intense about him and she didn't know why her parents couldn't see it. They were kind and expected everyone else to be kind as well, always seeming so shocked when they read the papers or heard the news. Her mother wouldn't listen to the radio because it upset her. They were always looking for ways to help other people, and Jasmine could see that Tim was just their latest project. They were determined to try to change the world one person at a time again.

Jasmine slipped out of the kitchen and went back to her room. She decided to shower, partly because she hadn't already that day and partly to cool down. They were in the midst of a heatwave, which always filled her with a certain amount of excitement but also dread. Considering her family spent every summer south of the equator, the heat shouldn't have been an issue. Maybe it wasn't the heat that was getting to her after all, but the presence of a stranger in their house.

When her parents told her they were getting a lodger this wasn't what she had expected. She wondered how long he planned to stay. There was something about him she didn't trust.

Chapter Three

Over the next few days Jasmine settled in to her new home, the smell of fresh paint gradually replaced by the smell of the musky perfume her mother wore and the shampoos and soaps they used. It was starting to smell like home. Jasmine had tinkered with her room, putting up a *Donnie Darko* poster. She hadn't seen the film, but her friend Felicity had given her the poster. She tacked it on the back of the door, where her parents wouldn't see it. They weren't controlling, but Frank and Lisa were such positive people that they really didn't understand Jasmine's fascination with morbid things. Lisa always said if you surrounded yourself with negativity then negative things would happen to you. Jasmine wasn't sure the world worked like that.

Their first home-cooked meal together in the new house was Pabellón Criollo, after living off Chinese food from the takeaway around the corner for the first few days after moving. Lisa made the Venezuelan dish especially for Jasmine, knowing it was her favourite, and the aroma of spicy beef filled the house, invoking childhood memories.

The dining table in the kitchen still had flecks of paint and pen stains from Jasmine's many school projects and artistic endeavours over the years, spending Sunday afternoons with Lisa painting by numbers or making quilled jewellery. Frank's idea of father-daughter bonding was taking her on fishing weekends in Wales, making her watch as he caught, gutted and cooked fish from the River Dee. As Jasmine had grown, however, she and her parents had spent less and less time doing these things together.

As Jasmine finished off her second plate of Pabellón Criollo, Tim appeared at the doors to the guest house. She had her back to the outside but she noticed the expression on her mother's face change to a smile, and her cheeks flush ever so slightly. Anyone who didn't know her mother like Jasmine did wouldn't think anything of it and it was clear Frank was oblivious as he carried on eating, totally focused on the food. She carefully turned her head to watch as Tim crossed the garden towards the house, then she turned and looked at her mother who quickly changed her expression when she caught Jasmine's eye. It was too late, though. Jasmine knew that her mother liked him. The uneasiness Jasmine had been feeling since Tim's arrival felt justified in that moment. It was Lisa who had convinced Frank that they needed a lodger, and it was Lisa who had suggested Tim.

'Sorry to bother you while you're having dinner. I just wondered if I could borrow a pan to heat some soup up in. I'll go shopping in the morning and grab one of my own. I didn't think about it earlier.'

'Don't be silly, why don't you have dinner with us? Welcome you into the fold and all that. I've made some spicy South American food.'

'I'm sure he just wants to settle in for now. Don't badger him,' Frank said.

'Nonsense, we have plenty of food. Come and sit, Tim.'

'It smells delicious, Lisa, thank you,' Tim said.

Tim came and sat at the table at Lisa's insistence, and she served him the last of the Pabellón Criollo, which Jasmine resented a little, even though she had already had seconds. Jasmine tried not to stare at him, but there really was something about him that set her teeth on edge. For the most part he continued to ignore her.

She couldn't figure him out, but there was something very off about Tim. Jasmine felt as though he had engineered this, like he wanted to be here in this room with them. Like he was trying to get closer to them, to be part of the family. Jasmine knew her parents tried to think the best of everyone though – they often said that the world would be a better place if everyone just tried to make one person's life better – but she sometimes wished they weren't so trusting. She would keep an eye on Tim. She would have to – no one else was going to.

Chapter Four

Now

I push down on my suitcase, trying to zip it closed. I remember the last time I used it how annoying it was and I make a mental note to throw it away after this journey. I have made this same mental note several times in the past but as soon as I return home I put it away and forget about it.

I can't stop thinking about the missing girl. I need to be there. I fear if I don't go then she will never be found, like the girl who went missing when I was younger.

I hear Chris in the next room putting Lloyd to bed. I know I should do it as I am the one who is leaving but I just want to get on the road. I think this time apart will be good for us – for me, anyway. I need to be a better wife, a better mother. Maybe going back there will make me realise how far I have come. I can barely remember the person I used to be. It's like I have been running for so long and trying to be different from my own mother that I have completely lost myself. It's hard to be a good example when you barely feel like a person at all.

'I don't understand why you have to leave right now. At least wait 'til morning. We can have a nice breakfast. You can't check in to your hotel until the afternoon anyway,' Chris says.

'I booked the hotel from today so I can check in as soon as I get there.'

'I see. You just can't wait to get out of here, can you?'

'Don't be like that. I wish I could explain it to you, but I can't.'

'This again? You think you're the only person who had a rotten childhood, but you aren't.'

'I'm not saying that, I never said that.'

'Then tell me what the big deal is. Why can't you just wait until Friday when I can come, too?'

'I will tell you, just not now. Please just let me do this on my own.'

'I don't know why I even try sometimes. You

are so immovable. You had better do some serious thinking while you're gone. If this isn't what you want, then cut us loose. I can't do this anymore.'

I try not to think about what it is he is actually saying. I know he's right. I know I can't be like this and expect everyone else to just be OK with it, for everyone to just carry on around me as if it isn't obvious I'm on the brink of falling apart. If he knew the truth about me, he might understand why I need to go back. I might be the best chance that girl has.

I go to Chris, his eyes glistening with emotion. I know I'm hurting him but I can't think about that right now, not with what's at stake. I kiss him and I can feel him exhale with relief, as if all he wanted was for me to tell him I still love him. Of course I do, that has never been in question. Not for me anyway.

'Come with the kids on Friday, if I'm not back already. Please.'

'Are you sure?'

'Of course. I love you, I hope you know that.'

'Sometimes I wonder.'

I pull away, not willing to play the guilt game anymore. I just need to get on the road. The sooner I leave the sooner I can get the answers I'm looking for. I feel the invisible thread as I am pulled back. My life so far has been in two parts, before and after, then and now. I think back to that summer. It feels like a lifetime ago, another world entirely. I put my case in the boot of the car. I never do this, I never drive far on my own, I never stay away from home without Chris or the kids. This will be the first time I have spent the night away from Lloyd. He's only seven, I hope he understands, I hope Chris does too, eventually. I have no choice. The life of that missing girl may depend on it.

Chapter Five

As I leave the safety of our little town in The Lake District, close to the border with Scotland, and head south, I feel a familiar dread wash over me. My knuckles whiten as I grip the steering wheel, almost clinging on for my life. I want to turn back, to pretend I didn't hear the news report, to carry on living inside my lies. I don't work, not really. I was young when Daisy was born and Chris thought it was better if I stayed home and looked after her. I've been with Chris my entire adult life; I knew from the moment we met that I would be safe with him. I feel bad again for leaving him with the children, especially when he is at such a crucial point in building his start-up business. Chris is in the process of trying to secure funding to convert a load of freight containers into affordable carbon-neutral houses, at first in the Lakes and then, if the model works, to a wider market.

Leaving late has its advantages and the roads are mostly clear. There is a little rain but it's not enough to break the humidity and not enough to make me pull over. I hate driving in the rain but it feels appropriate somehow. My thoughts focus on what awaits me in Devon. I realise then that I didn't eat lunch or dinner today, too consumed with organising the family so I could get away and deal with this.

I pull over at a service station – it's properly dark now – as I am so hungry I can barely concentrate. I grab a sandwich and take it to the seating area. The rain gets heavier outside and I pull my coat around me. It's not cold but I feel strange being here by myself. A man sits at my table and smiles at me. There are plenty of empty seats so I don't understand why he's chosen that seat, or why he's looking at me.

'Can I help you?'

'Thought you might be lonely sitting here.'

'Well I'm not.'

I had forgotten about this, not going out much, not being part of the world but staying in my safe little village with my family and all the familiar faces of neighbours and acquaintances. I forgot that sometimes people – strangers – just come and speak to you. I feel the panic rising in me. I want him to go away but I don't want to upset him as I don't know what he might do. Of course he is probably just lonely, but that doesn't give him the right to bother me. He opens his mouth but I stand and move to another table. I can hear Chris in my ear telling me not to be rude, not to be unfriendly. I finish my sandwich quickly and go and buy some cola to drink on the ride, full sugar to keep me awake.

As I make my way to the car, I look behind me to see the man from the café following me. I put my hand in my bag to find the keys, putting them between my fingers when I do. The service station is strangely quiet and I feel unsafe. The car is close now but somehow I feel like I'm getting further away. Behind me I hear the beep of a car alarm being turned off and the sound of a door opening. As I reach my own car I turn and see the man who was following me pulling out of a spot and driving towards the exit. I get in and lock the doors, feeling stupid. I wish I was at home with Chris and the kids, I wish I didn't have to do this alone. I pull myself together and start the car before pulling back out onto the motorway. I'm on a collision course with the ghosts of my past and there is nothing I can do to stop it. This road somehow feels like the purgatory between my real life now – the one where I am safe and loved – and the mess I left behind.

I change the radio station regularly as I drive, with little tolerance for anything for a prolonged period of time. I finally reach a local Devonshire radio station and my blood runs cold – I'm getting closer. My head begins to throb. I open the glove box and root around for pills of some kind. I usually keep a packet or two in there. I find a pack with just two left and I knock them back with my Coke, even though I know they won't take the thrumming in my temples away. Nothing will until I am out of this place, until I am on my way home. Inside I already feel like I am never going to get home, that I got lucky the last time I left this place, reluctantly released from its grip into the world with the proviso that I never return. I'm breaking a pact I made with myself sixteen years ago when I first got on that bus out of town. I promised I would never go back. I told the universe that if it just let me get away then I would be a good person, if that was even possible for someone like me.

The road signs become increasingly familiar as I approach my destination. I see houses and streets from my childhood. It's like walking through that wardrobe and into Narnia – another world entirely, one I am not supposed to be in, one that's not meant for me. It's too late now. There is no turning back.

Chapter Six

Time has stopped here. I am glad that the world is sleeping when I finally drive through the winding valley and the crossroads that lead into the actual town. I have walked these pavements until my feet were sore in the past. I'm hit with a wave of nostalgia I wasn't expecting. I left abruptly and have never made my peace with it, my mind writing the town and its inhabitants off the second I was a few miles away, desperate to forget all of the things that happened, good or bad. The memories come flooding in, something I was afraid of. I drive past a bus stop that I remember sitting in with school friends and a bottle of cider, a smile creeping across my face as I remember a part of my life that I have kept buried for the longest time. I see the turning for a road where we used to live and feel every muscle in my body tense, thankful that I don't need to drive past the house to get to where I need to go.

Further into the town is the old cinema, just past my family's dentist. I see the ghost of myself on every corner. I had forgotten how much of me was shaped in this town. The cinema looks the same, as do the shops surrounding it. How can so much time have passed outside this town and yet nothing has changed on the inside? To me the town is alive, a monster in my mind, dark and insidious, creeping and malevolent. I feel its fingers around me, gently pulling me in, leading me towards a place I am not sure I want to go. I have always thought that this town isn't like anywhere else, that once it gets a hold of you, you can't escape, almost as if some ancient pagan magic is at work. I know it makes no sense, but I think of it almost as if it were a person who had wronged me, someone I can never forgive, someone I am afraid to let into my heart again. So instead I just feel anger towards it. As if these buildings and streets are all complicit somehow.

I can feel the sea before I see it. Something always feels different about coastal towns, as if they are on the edge of the world somehow. There is no way to get lost as long as you can find the sea. I am glad I drove here at night. I didn't tell Chris it was because I didn't want to have to look at the people who live here as I drove past them, wondering if I knew them, wondering if they knew me. I just want to get inside the hotel and close the door, giving myself a few hours before I have to venture out again. Taking off was unusually selfish of me, but from the moment I saw that news report I knew there was nothing else I could do. I have to find out what happened. The locals will know things that aren't in the news. I'll find out who the missing girl is, why she was here and what happened to her. For some reason I think I'm the only one who can.

I pull into the hotel car park, the huge red brick building a monument to a different time. I could have chosen a less expensive hotel, but this is the one we used to look at and wonder what was inside, it always seemed so posh and decadent. Standing in front of it now, it seems much smaller than I remember, much less imposing. It's still grand but it's dated, and not in a good way. I feel like an imposter just stepping through the doors, as if I'm not actually allowed to be in this building, as if it knows who I am.

I approach the desk, studying the face of the woman behind the counter. It's a small town and

I half expect her to recognise me even though I don't recognise her. That is, until she opens her mouth to speak.

'Hello, Miss, how can I help you?' she says. Her accent is French or Belgian, or something like that. I feel instant relief that she isn't local.

'I called ahead to say I would be arriving tonight. I'm a little later than I expected.'

'Mrs Felicity Musgrave?'

'Yes.'

She has the paperwork ready. I sign the card and she shares the Wi-Fi password. She explains that I am too late to order breakfast to my room in the morning, but I can eat in the dining room with the other guests, or I can order room service from a limited menu at any point during my stay. I am so tired I can barely decipher what she is saying and the speed at which she speaks doesn't make things any easier. But I smile and nod at the correct intervals and she finally hands me the key. She gestures to a porter to come and take my bag. I follow him dutifully, embarrassed now that I booked this place, embarrassed that I am making someone carry my bag. I was proving a point to myself and no one else, that I'm a better person now than I was when I left. All the money in the world can't wash away the things I did though.

My room overlooks the beach. I can see what

they mean when they say it's darkest just before dawn. The sea is a sheet of black. The room itself was probably considered very opulent a few years ago, but now it gives off the impression that lots of hotel rooms do; that lots of people have slept there. I know that within a few hours, though, this will be the only place in the whole town where I feel even remotely comfortable.

I pull out my phone to text Chris. It's unusual for me to open my phone and not find a supportive message from him there, although in recent months I have noticed a change in the way he is with me. He's been less tolerant of my idiosyncrasies lately and it's as if I want to push him even further, to see how far I can before he stops loving me. I miss him. I can tell he is unhappy because I have no notifications at all. I just message the word 'here' along with a kiss and turn my phone off. For now I want to sleep.

I brush my teeth, desperate to get rid of the sugary coating from the Coke I had in the car. I look at my reflection for what feels like the first time in days and wipe the heavy black liner from my top lid and what remains of my red lipstick. It's one of those lipsticks that lasts for hours. I'm not even sure why I put it on for the journey. Habit, I suppose. I don't go anywhere without my war paint on. I pull my hair into a ponytail on top of my head and wash my face, then I mois-turise. My little routines are often what get me through when my anxiety starts to creep to the surface – which is why social situations are so hard; I don't have a routine for those.

The bed is huge, a super king I suspect, and just magnifies my loneliness as I climb in, sticking to the left hand side because that's where I always sleep. I try to shuffle to the middle but it just feels wrong somehow. I put my phone on the bedside table even though it's off and I lie down and count backwards from a hundred in my head. It's a method I contrived to stop myself from thinking too much before I fall asleep, otherwise the night terrors come and those are something you never quite get accustomed to. In the back of my mind I can see faces from my past that I have tried to forget so I concentrate on the numbers.

Seventy-eight. Seventy-seven. Seventy-six. Seventy-five. I see hands claw at me for help but I pull away. Seventy-four. Seventy-three. Seventy-two. I watch helplessly as the sea swallows them. Seventy-one. Seventy. Sixty-nine. Sixty-eight. I stand for a moment at the cliff's edge and watch for them to reappear, but it never happens. I close my eyes tighter and focus harder on the numbers. Sixty-seven. Sixty-six. Sixty-five. Stop thinking. *Please stop thinking . . .*

Chapter Seven

Then

It turned out that Jasmine's parents knew Tim from when Lisa worked in the shelter last year. Tim was homeless and staying with the Burgesses for a while until he got back on his feet. He was going to work on the Burgess house in return for a reduced rent. Until then, Tim had painted elderly people's homes in exchange for a hot meal. Since he'd started doing that, lots of people had paid him to do odd jobs for cash and he'd largely managed to turn his life around, though he'd been living out of his car until now.

Jasmine helped her father in the garage. They had both woken up at the crack of dawn, the sun already shining. They were putting all the boxes that didn't need to be unpacked just yet in there. Considering they had moved from a smaller house it was amazing how much stuff they had brought with them.

'Can Flick come over when you go away next weekend?'

'She's always welcome here, I hope she knows that.'

'I suppose Tim will be around as well?' she said, almost spitting his name.

'I don't know what you've got against him. Has he said anything to upset you?'

'No, he hasn't said anything. It's not that. Don't you think he's weird?'

'People say I'm weird, Jasmine, doesn't make me a bad guy. No one besides you has a bad word to say about him. He's done a lot of good things for people for no payment. He's ex-military so I know we can trust him. This is no different to us helping the people when we go abroad. Charity begins at home, Jasmine.'

Jasmine handed her father another box to put on the shelf. She knew when her parents got it into their minds to help someone there was no deterring them. She just resented not being consulted on something that would impact her life just as much as theirs.

'Why isn't *he* doing this then if he's so brilliant? I thought he was staying to help around the house.'

'He's not going to be our personal slave, Jasmine. You can't spare twenty minutes away from the television to stack a couple of boxes?'

'He's just always there, you know? He's not very approachable either.'

'Sometimes when people are afraid or shy, they can appear a bit awkward. He's been through a lot and it's our duty to help him. You're just projecting when you say things like that. I think you're feeling guilty for being unfriendly. You're being a bit selfish and unreasonable and I'm not sure I like this side of you. We didn't bring you up like that. I'd suggest you make more of an effort because he's staying and you need to get used to it.'

'Fine.'

She knew better than to push the point with her father. He was a small man but he could be fierce when he wanted to.

'Pass me the fishing rods and you can go back to whatever you were doing before I disturbed you. I've got to get off to work anyway.'

Jasmine found it hard to believe that the person her father was talking about was the man living in their guest house. There was no warmth about him at all. But her parents weren't the kind of

41

people who took risks, so they must have been pretty sure about Tim to let him live with them.

Jasmine's room caught the sun for most of the day, and even with the curtains drawn the heat seeped in. She was tired that morning because she'd stayed up late reading a true crime book about women who killed. She found things like that fascinating, but her parents hated that she was into the macabre so she tried to read when they weren't around. She wanted to read another chapter but it was just too warm in there and there probably wasn't enough time before she went to school anyway.

Jasmine had just settled in the kitchen with a bowl of muesli and her summer art project – meant to build her portfolio for college – when Tim knocked on one of the French doors. She felt she had no choice but to nod that it was OK for him to come in, remembering that her father had told her to be nice to him. So far, Jasmine had no reason to question her father's judgement of character and if he trusted Tim then she had to as well.

'Your dad told me he wanted me to work on the lounge today. Do you mind if I get started now?'

'Why would I mind?' Jasmine asked, a little more aggressive than necessary.

'I just don't want to disturb anyone. Is your dad here?'

'No, he left for work already. Mum's still in bed,' she replied, wondering if she shouldn't have let him in after all.

Tim looked up as though he could see through the floor into her parents' room. When there was no movement from upstairs, he relaxed a little, the deep furrow in his brow disappearing as he pulled a dining chair out and sat opposite Jasmine, almost reclining, his backside on the edge of the seat and one leg stretched out in front of him.

'What you drawing?'

'If you can't tell then I'm doing it wrong,' Jasmine said flippantly. She saw him smile and it was like looking at a different man; softer somehow, kinder.

He placed his palms on the table then stood and leaned over, tilting his head to look at the drawing. She couldn't take his eyes off his forearms; they were strong and tan and still sported those tiny white flecks. From this distance she could hear him breathing.

'Is it the fruit bowl?' he asked, still leaning over, his face just inches from Jasmine's. She made the mistake of looking up and their eyes locked. For the first time she noticed his eyes properly; they were grey with a deep blue ring around the outside.

Her pulse quickened, but Tim broke eye contact first and slumped back in the seat, taking the apple from the top of the bowl, the one she was sketching. She was drawn to his mouth as he bit into the apple, his lips moistening with the juice. She snapped her eyes away and stood up. Jasmine left her soggy muesli on the table, grabbed her art homework and stuffed it into her bag, suddenly wanting to get out of the house. When she looked back he was smiling, a different kind of smile this time. He pulled her bowl of muesli over and started to eat it.

Chapter Eight

At dinner that night, Jasmine's parents talked about the group they usually went away with for the summer holidays. Guyana had been picked as their destination this year. Jasmine had never been there before. It was never much of a holiday for her family, if she was honest, as they went to do charitable work in underprivileged communities. Both of her parents saved up their annual leave and they usually stayed for several weeks and helped with the completion of a charity project – they'd been every year since before Jasmine was born. This year they couldn't go, though, because her father had had hip replacement surgery earlier that summer and the doctor had advised against a long-haul flight. Jasmine knew he was devastated to cause them to miss their trip. He had always been so active and full of energy that she felt sorry for him. He had spent several months in pain before finally conceding to going in for the operation and his posture hadn't seemed to have recovered. It hadn't helped that he had a fear of hospitals that they didn't really talk about, something from his childhood that had left an emotional scar. This was the first time she had really considered his age; seen the way his stature had changed in just the last year. He wasn't a tall man to begin with and he had lost a little weight so it seemed he'd almost shrunk somehow.

'How's your drama club going? What's the big play that you're doing this year?' Frank said, asking the obligatory parental questions about her interests.

'Drama is going well. I might even get a part in the college production of *A Midsummer Night's Dream* this year, what with us not going away. Lots of rehearsals going on over the summer.'

'Oh, that's exciting,' her mother said in a way that made Jasmine think she wasn't particularly excited at all. They loved travelling all over the globe and this would be the first summer that Jasmine could remember staying at home. She could tell both her parents were deeply disappointed about this.

'Because I'm here for the rehearsals over the summer, Miss Cotterel said I should audition for the role of Titania, the fairy queen. I said I would happily help with the set design as well. The production isn't until Christmas but because I already have a place on the drama A Level I can attend the auditions in August,' Jasmine said, rubbing it in a little. Normally Jasmine's interests came last. Not this time though; this time she could do all the summery things that had been denied to her in previous years. She knew her friend Felicity was jealous of all the places she had been and all the experiences she had had, yet she had prayed something would happen to stop them from travelling. She felt responsible for her father getting sick, as if his illness was somehow a manifestation of her resentful thoughts.

'That's wonderful, Jasmine, I'm proud,' her mother said, and her father nodded his approval.

'Is Felicity doing the play?'

'Yes. Actually, I wanted to ask if you would mind giving her a lift to rehearsals with me and dropping her off.'

'She still having problems at home?'

'You know what her mum's like.'

'She's back drinking then?'

'She's got a new boyfriend who is a complete nightmare apparently. Flick doesn't like being there.'

'Well, she is always welcome here as much as she wants over the summer. Poor girl.'

Jasmine smiled to herself at the thought of all the fun she and Felicity could have over the break. She couldn't help but feel guilty for being glad to be home this year. She had met so many people with much less than her who were more than content with their lives, happy even. Jasmine thought of the tobacco ladies in the tiny village in Peru. They would get paid to sit all day in the blistering heat, threading tobacco leaves onto a long string which would then be hung to dry in large rickety wooden sheds. Her family had visited the village when she was nine years old and she had made friends with the girls from the local area. They often went to sit with the tobacco ladies and help thread the leaves onto the string. A full day's work there was brutal, the big flat needle often cutting or stabbing your fingers. The seasoned workers had yellow calloused hands and the smell of fresh tobacco permeated every item of clothing Jasmine wore on those days. There were very young girls working there too, younger than her, day in day out, in August heat. Jasmine wondered if some of those little girls she saw threading tobacco with their grandmothers were still working there today.

'Did you see what Tim's done in the lounge?' Lisa said to Frank.

'No, is it good?'

'It's not finished yet, but it's going to be. He's built low level cupboards in the alcove.'

'I always wanted to be a carpenter. Maybe I should get Tim to teach me,' Frank said.

'We should see if we can interest him in coming away with us next year. A man with his skills could cut the building time of our projects in half.'

'We hardly know him,' Jasmine said, concerned with how quickly her parents were incorporating Tim into every aspect of their lives. Her parents' mention of 'next year' made it sound like they were planning on making him a permanent fixture. Even though they had travelled all over the world they could be quite naive sometimes about people and their intentions. Jasmine had seen them get hurt before when they trusted the wrong people. She hoped they weren't wrong about Tim. For all of their sakes.

'Well, we don't want to put that kind of pressure on him anyway. Especially when he is doing us such a huge favour.'

'How is he doing us a favour?' Jasmine asked, trying to keep the snark out of her voice.

'He's going to fit our new kitchen for us – it's costing us about a quarter of what it would if we used a professional kitchen fitter. The things we want done in the house would take years and years to save for, so Tim really is a godsend.'

'But you're letting him live here,' Jasmine pointed out.

'And he's paying us.'

'With the money *you're* paying him. How does that make sense?'

'When you have a house and children of your own, you will understand how much things cost. He's also continuing his work with the charity in town and doing jobs for elderly people. We really want to help him out. Charity begins at home. I'm surprised at you, Jasmine,' her mother said, her pride in Jasmine disappearing.

'I'm sorry. I think I'm just really tired. School was a bit hectic today,' Jasmine said sheepishly, trying to win her mother's approval again. She hated disappointing either one of her parents. The older she got the more it seemed to happen.

'What if Tim had heard you?' Frank asked disapprovingly. Jasmine could see that she was outnumbered. 'I want you to make an effort to be nice to him, he's a good guy.'

'Look, I know why you're nervous – it's because of what happened at school. Not all men are like that,' Lisa said, reaching across the table to comfort Jasmine, but she pulled her hand away from her mother.

They just wouldn't let her forget about the incident.

'So, because of what happened last year I don't know what I'm talking about? Don't I deserve a little more credit than that? You want me to be more mature but then you treat me like a child.'

'You can't just go around being suspicious of everyone, Jasmine. He hasn't done anything to warrant this attitude from you. He deserves a chance, at least.'

'I guess my feelings matter less than the feelings of some stranger you've just let move in with us.'

'That's enough,' Frank said in a voice that indicated he was done talking. He rarely snapped at Jasmine but she knew enough to know that she had lost this argument.

'I'm tired, I'm going to bed,' Jasmine told them and stood up quickly, the chair making the angry scream she wished she could.

'Jasmine! Come back!' her mother called after her, but she was already halfway up the stairs.

Chapter Nine

Now

I wake up confused, slightly panicked at my unfamiliar surroundings before I remember where I am. I am still on my side of the bed, still locked in my old routine. I look at the clock and see that it's after lunch. Without the children or Chris to tend to I feel aimless. I go to the window and look out towards the seafront and see the people walking from the centre up towards Jacob's Ladder. It's weird being this side of the looking glass. I glance at my phone and see Chris hasn't called. He's still annoyed at me, but what can I do? I have spent more than a decade just being available, changing my plans to accommodate his deadlines, having nothing better to do. Well, for once I have something better to do.

After my shower I put on a grey summer dress that touches the floor when I walk. I feel very monochrome with my black hair and white sandals. I add my trademark red lipstick – I feel uncomfortable without it and it pulls the outfit together – and I take a small bottle of vodka from the minibar and drink it. I need some courage before I venture outside.

I completely missed breakfast and so my first task is to find some food. I decide to walk via The Triangle, where the main bus terminal for the town is located. That was the last place the missing girl was seen. There won't be anything there but it's as good a place as any to start. The closer I get to my destination the more my stomach turns. I walk up the road past the Bedford Hotel and The Triangle comes into view. Nothing has changed about it. It's strange how you can spend so long away from a place but still know it so well. I sit on the wall opposite the actual terminal and watch the buses come and go, the drivers a mix of men and women. The drivers were all very familiar with us kids, going up to town and back hundreds of times a week. There was one old driver who would offer the girls free bus rides if they would touch his crotch. As far as I know, no one ever did, but that didn't stop him from asking. We all referred to him as Pervy Pete and that was all there was to it. No big deal. The thought of my Daisy dealing with guys like that really makes my skin crawl but she is the same age as I was back then; it would be naive of me to think she lives in a bubble of innocence.

I keep my head down as I watch people gather at the stop, waiting for the next bus, all ignoring each other even though they probably get the same bus together day in, day out. The discomfort of proximity in a small town. I wonder what the people I used to know in school would look like now – would I even remember them? I hope they don't remember me. I wasn't what you would call popular and if the people I used to know are anything like me they will barely remember their friendship group, let alone anyone outside of it.

There are no cameras here at The Triangle and so it's unlikely that there is any lead on who took the girl, what kind of vehicle, or exactly what time. Her name was Mandy Green and she was fifteen years old, the same age as my Daisy. Did she get in a car with someone she knew, or was it just an opportunistic drive-by kidnapping? I remembered reading on the local news website that one bus driver saw her there waiting for a bus, but when the next bus arrived she was gone. There are a few bunches of flowers tied to the railings, which I find odd. The girl wasn't dead, or at least they hadn't found a body. Who put the flowers on the railings? I am too scared to go and look at the flowers in case there is a note. There is one name I am scared of seeing. How much do the police actually know? The thought that he might be here again is too much to bear. Did he come back for me? No – it must be someone else, but why? And why is it so similar? Maybe I'm over-reacting; maybe the girl has just run away. Where the hell was Mandy? The voice in the back of my head tells me I did the right thing by coming here. I remember standing in this same spot all those years ago and wondering what had happened to the girl who disappeared, the girl who could have been me, could have been any of us. I have so many questions that I never dared ask, questions I never thought I would get answers for. I'm still too afraid to even think of what the answers might be.

I get up and walk towards the church and then proceed down the uneven pavement on Church Hill into the market square. I see the butcher's is still there and the baker's, a chocolate shop I don't remember and also a shop filled with luxury Christmas decorations. Only in a town like this would a business like that be viable in July. There was a lot of money among some of the older residents and Christmas was an inevitability that they looked forward to, often because it might be their last.

I thought as soon as I returned that people would be pointing at me and whispering, but that isn't happening. It feels like most of the people walking around are just visiting for the day. If I didn't know what I know, I would think it was a beautiful place, the kind of place I would aspire to live in one day.

I go to a small tea room and order a sandwich. It feels like a living room, the walls covered in a flocked wallpaper smattered with little photo frames and inspirational quotes on small tapestries. It's not the sort of place I would have ventured into when I was a teenager.

'Has this place been here long?' I ask the proprietor when she puts my food in front of me.

'We took it over about twelve years ago, but the previous owners were here for a long time before that. Before that I think it used to be a hairdresser's. Where are you from then?' She answers me with far more information than I expected and a question thrown in just to spike my anxiety.

'Just visiting from The Lake District.'

'Oh, I'd love to go there, it's beautiful. You visiting family here?'

'No, my family is all back in the Lakes, I just fancied a getaway,' I lie, trying to appear like a person who would just take a holiday on their own for the experience, not like someone who gets an anxiety attack even having to leave the house to post a letter.

'Oh, well, it's lovely here, too. You staying local?'

'Yes, at the Victoria.' I feel a little embarrassed as I say it, as if I am showing off. I notice a slight change in her expression; I have a feeling she thinks less of me now. Maybe that's what I wanted.

'You here on your own then?'

'My husband is joining me with the kids at the weekend,' I say, kicking myself for giving anything about myself away. I change the subject quickly. 'I heard about that girl that went missing.'

'Oh gosh yes, that was awful. They haven't found her yet. It's been a few days so I doubt they will either.'

'Did you know her?'

She shakes her head.

'She wasn't local then?'

'She lived up Manston way and the family were a little weird. Just her and her mum, I think. They only moved back to the town a year or so ago, but I think the mum was originally from round this way.'

A year would be considered very new to the

area. If people could say what age you were when you moved here, they'd hold it against you. I remembered a Polish boy who joined at the beginning of secondary and no one let him forget it. He was the 'new kid' until someone newer came along, which wasn't until four years later.

I turn away from her and start to eat my sandwich. I didn't think she'd have even this much information for me. The news made it sound like Mandy was a tourist, but she was local.

I can't help but think of Daisy when I am here. I was her age when I lived here, when I left. The person I am now was moulded back then, from the events that I witnessed, the things I ran away from. I'm hit with fresh guilt over the kind of mother I am, over the fact that I left them to come here and chase ghosts. I promised I would be better than the mother I had, and I have been, but the bar was very low, underground even. When you have your own children it's much easier to question your own parents' choices and not just blindly follow them. You realise the precious life you are responsible for looks to you for guidance, for direction.

I realise if I want to get answers then I need to actually go and look for them. I only eat half of the food, my appetite gone, then put a ten-pound note on the table – which more than covers my bill – before leaving the tea room. I walk back to the bus stop and get on a bus, the driver a woman, something you didn't see very often when I lived here. There is no one else on board and so I sit at the front. There are a few minutes to wait and the driver stands just outside the door having a cigarette.

'Excuse me,' I say, and she turns to me in surprise, as though no one has ever done this before.

'I'll take your money in a minute.' She smiles awkwardly and continues to smoke.

'Oh no, I just wanted to ask if you knew anything about that girl that went missing. They said she was last seen at this bus stop.'

'Yeah, terrible business, poor girl.'

'Did you know her?'

'Seen her on the bus a few times, but no, I didn't know her. She was a quiet little thing, very polite though, unlike some of the little scrotes round here.'

'Do you know who saw her last?'

'Yeah, it was Bill Hawkins, drives the Honiton bus. Said she was in the hut when he pulled off. Next bus to come along was one of these, the driver said she weren't there then.'

'Was there a long wait? Could she have decided to walk?'

'Someone would have seen her on the road,

unless she went up the back way I suppose. But the hotel on the road up there has CCTV pointed at their car park and it catches the pavement. The local paper said no one walked up that way.'

'What was her surname again?' I ask, trying to cover the fact that I have asked so many odd questions with something a little more obvious.

'You're not a reporter, are you? Asking all these questions?' the woman said with a raised eyebrow, maybe teasing, maybe not.

'Oh gosh no, just curious in case I know her family. Wouldn't want to put my foot in it,' I say, realising I must sound odd asking.

'Her name is Mandy Green. Her mum Liz works up at the Spar shop on Temple Street, although I haven't seen her there since it happened.'

I want to recognise the name, to justify my being here – but Mandy Green still means nothing to me. I try to think of anyone I might have known back then with that name, but I have done such a good job of suppressing my past that I draw a blank. Something tells me the girl is connected to me. I just don't know how.

'Thank you,' I say as she puts the cigarette out and gets on the bus. I move back so she can get into her cab and put a five pound note on her tray. I can't remember the last time I was on a bus for anything.

'Where you off to?'

'Just up to the fork please. Single,' I say. It's only a short walk from there to the Spar. Even though there's a bus stop outside the shop I don't want the driver to know I'm going straight there.

She prints out the ticket and gives me my change and I retreat to the back of the bus. It has leather seats and is much cleaner than I ever remember these buses being. Maybe I'm judging this town too harshly – maybe my whole view is tarnished by my own experiences. We go past several houses I remember visiting at one point or another, although I can't remember who lived there. Before I know it, I am off the bus again. I stand at the fork in the road, very aware of how close I am to my old house. The Spar was my local newsagent for a while; my mother would send me there for milk and I would complain because it was uphill all the way home. I look at the houses that surround me, the faded pastel paint and mossy trails around the foundations as though they had been steeped in algae. The gardens were the real prize, bursts of coloured blooms and a multitude of greens, like something out of a fairy tale. They look exactly as I remember them, almost as if I'm looking at a photograph of the past. That's the thing about these old towns, changes were hard won because no one wanted them.

I stand outside the shop and take a few deep breaths. Maybe Liz Green could shed some light on what happened to her daughter, her daughter who is just a few weeks older than mine. I try not to think about Daisy. I like to think she would have been safe if I had stayed here, but even that makes me feel guilty. Guilty that I was never a target.

I walk into the shop and browse the snacks, picking up several bags of chocolates and crisps to eat in the hotel room, enough for several weeks, theoretically. I tell myself I can give some to the kids when they come at the weekend, but I know they won't last that long. I grab several cans of premixed gin and tonic; I don't want Chris to be able to keep tabs on how much I drink in my room from the hotel minibar bill. They replenish it every day when the cleaners fix the room. I must try to stay away from it. I always have a bottle of something hidden at home, too, for the same reason. He worries about my anxieties and the way I deal with them, which makes me keep secrets from him. If I'm being honest, I'm not sure Chris even knows me at all – all he gets is what I give him, and I certainly don't give him much. I don't do it out of spite, I do it out of necessity, to survive. I can't be without him and if he knew the real me he would run and never look back.

I approach the counter and see a woman with thick glasses and short dark hair. Her nametag says Liz so I know she's the mother of the missing girl, but without that I wouldn't recognise her, although there is something familiar about her. I try not to judge her for being at work while her daughter is missing; I know she probably has no choice. Knowing where Liz lives has already influenced what I think of her. I hate that that's true, but it is. I am already imagining what kind of mother she is purely based on where she lives. Seeing her in person has only confirmed my prejudice. Liz looks hard, much older than she should, and as she removes my items from the basket and scans them I can see she's a heavy smoker; her fingers are a deep yellow and there are grooves all around her lips from years of sucking on cigarettes. I know my prejudices come from hearing my own mother speak about the people who lived in this neighbourhood. My mother had a lot of hypocritical opinions for someone who lived the life that she did.

'Are you the mother of the girl that went missing?' I feel compelled to be at least partially honest with her about what brought me here, as she deserves that. I am confident she won't remember me. She looks lost; she barely pays attention to my face at all.

'I am,' she says, staring past me, her eyes connecting with nothing.

'I just wanted to say sorry and I hope you find her soon,' I say as sincerely as I can, even though I don't believe they will find her – gone is gone.

'Thank you,' she says, placing her hand on mine for a moment and squeezing, making me feel guilty for even coming here. I see her eyes brim over and she dashes out to the back of the shop. Her colleague who was restocking a shelf nearby comes to finish serving me.

'Sorry, I didn't mean to upset her.'

'She shouldn't be back at work really, been doing that all morning,' the other lady says sympathetically. Her nametag says Charlotte.

'Do they have any idea where her daughter might be?'

'No. Someone I know who works at the Fort Hotel said they saw her getting into an old brown car but they couldn't confirm it, could have been another kid or another day. It's like she just up and vanished. Very strange business. That kind of thing just doesn't happen around here. There are tons of rumours flying around about what happened.'

'I heard it happened once before, about sixteen years ago.' I try to keep eye contact, not shift my eyes or look suspicious in any way, as if we are talking about a movie we saw, not something that matters, not something I was part of.

'What are the chances it's the same person? That they would wait sixteen years to do it again? That will be twenty-four pounds and eighty seven pence,' Liz's colleague Charlotte said.

I pay with contactless. 'I guess you're right, sixteen years is a long time to wait.'

'Was probably one of those fairground folk. I don't trust them,' Charlotte said.

'Is the fair still in town?'

'No, thank goodness. Packed up as soon as there was any sign of trouble. Shady bunch. Can I get you anything else?'

'No. Thank you.'

After I leave the newsagent's I decide to cut through to the park that leads towards town. There are lots of people out walking their dogs. No mutts in sight, all groomed and healthy-looking designer breeds like labradoodles and cockapoos. I feel torn between my contempt for the wealthy people in this town and my ingrained feeling of superiority over the people on the other side of that coin. I never did fit in here.

I think about the brown car that the woman mentioned. It couldn't be the same car, could it? Brown wasn't a particularly popular colour but what were the chances that it was *his* car? How could it be? And why now? Was he back? I should go to the police and tell them what I know, but the thought of it makes me feel sick. By doing so I could be taking a sledgehammer to the life I've constructed for myself. I would be pulled back into a world I only escaped by the skin of my teeth. Mandy can't still be alive, so I would be hurting myself for no reason. I walk as briskly as I can back to the hotel, afraid with every passing moment that someone will recognise me and the world will find out the truth. I would die before that happened.

Chapter Ten

Then

Jasmine sat in her room listening to music. She had hooked her desk chair under the doorknob because she didn't want to speak to her parents, and with her headphones on she wouldn't hear them if they knocked on the door anyway. She was still cross with her mother for bringing up what had happened at school last year.

Jasmine's English teacher Mr Morrell – who, for obvious reasons, no longer worked at the school – had tried to kiss Jasmine. He *had* kissed her. He had mistaken her general enthusiasm for the subject as something else.

Jasmine had joined all the after-school reading

clubs and the debate club which James Morrell ran. He thought Jasmine was trying to get closer to him because she was somehow attracted to him, but she just loved books. She had been reading *Jane Eyre* – a book partly about a girl who was in love with a much older man – and Mr Morrell had misread the signs and took her love of the book as something else and made a career-ending mistake. Frank and Lisa had explained in their usual charitable way that he was young and had not long been a teacher, so had blurred the lines between her love of the subject and her possible love for him.

He explained later – in a letter he was permitted to send Jasmine as part of her therapy – that he had thought she was flirting with him, that it was his mistake and she wasn't to blame for what he'd done. He'd apologised for any distress caused and said he hoped that she would get over it in time. Jasmine had felt betrayed – that he could think she was into him made the relationship she thought they had fake. He never really thought she had potential; his encouragement and support were a lie, a way to get to Jasmine. The most distressing part of that whole experience was what came after, though. Interviews and questions, counselling and sad puppy dog looks from everyone who treated Jasmine like some kind of victim. By the end of it she thought there was something wrong with her because she wasn't completely traumatised by the incident. A part of her wondered if she *had* done something to lead him on but if she had, it was unintentional. Jasmine did feel bad that he had lost his job, but she knew it wasn't her fault.

At the time, the incident had brought Jasmine closer to her parents, but since then they had babied her and been a little dismissive – anytime she was upset about something it was because of what happened with James Morrell. But were they right? Was Jasmine's unease around their new lodger just a reaction to what had happened last year? Jasmine didn't know if she could trust her own instincts, because she really hadn't seen it coming when Morrell kissed her.

And yet, she found herself aware of Tim in a way she'd never been aware of her teacher and that scared her. Was her mind playing tricks on her or was he really a threat? She had a feeling it wouldn't be long before she found out.

Chapter Eleven

Only two exams left before Jasmine finished school for the year. She hadn't yet decided whether to go to the sixth form college instead of staying at her school – technically she had been accepted into both – as it all depended on Felicity. They had come to rely on each other since becoming friends, and moving to a new school without her didn't feel like something Jasmine would ever want to do. They had agreed they both felt a bit limited in Sidmouth and it would be nice to get a bus into the city just for a change of scenery, a chance to meet different people instead of being stuck with the same people since primary school. The town was so small, dwarfed by the English Channel that ran alongside it and the Jurassic coastline that enveloped them.

After school Jasmine was going to walk into town with Felicity. A lot of the shops were independent and quirky, the council constantly fighting against the franchises that had swallowed every other town. As a result, the prices were less than ideal and so Jasmine and Felicity spent most of their pocket money buying clothes in the charity shops. The upside was that the clothes in the charity shops were often designer and much cheaper than the independent shops whose target audiences were women over fifty and people who owned boats. It wasn't a town for young people.

Jasmine liked it in Sidmouth, but she didn't feel she had a lot in common with anyone apart from Felicity and they barely had anything in common, not really. Felicity's home life was a mess; her mother drank and had a revolving-door policy on boyfriends. Jasmine was both jealous of Felicity and fiercely protective of her; she was the only real friend she had. She wondered if that had something to do with her family's summers abroad. She didn't usually get to spend the holiday roaming the streets and discovering new hangouts or even hanging out in the old ones. The worst thing was missing the folk festival. Almost all of her school friends' summer stories came from that one week in August. The town transformed into a hive of activity, people coming from all over the world to visit the sleepy little place. Jasmine had been there for one day of it before and it was like being in another place entirely. There were street performers and Morris dancers everywhere you looked. Extortionately expensive tie-dyed clothing and lots of multicultural and vegan food stalls dotted the streets. She was happy she was going to be around for it this year, and she felt guilty for that. For the first time, her summer would be normal.

Felicity came from another school entirely a few years ago and Jasmine had sort of adopted her. Everyone else had their own cliques formed from primary school but the two girls drifted between them. They weren't an obvious choice for best friends but somehow it worked. Felicity loved to tell Jasmine all the things she had missed over the summer, all the boys she got off with. Jasmine thought in part she was jealous of her adventures, but Jasmine was so much more jealous of Felicity's adventures at home.

Jasmine got along with everyone at school, but it was because no one really knew her, no one took the time. Maybe that was why she threw herself into books, maybe that was why Mr Morrell thought she was interested in him; because she spent time with him instead of friends. The truth was, she didn't have any real friends aside from Felicity, who was heavily involved in lots of sports clubs, anything to keep her late at school, anything to keep her from going home.

When her geography exam was finally over – they had different exams as they took different subjects for their options – Felicity met Jasmine at the gate. As they walked into town it started to spit, the temperature cooling ever so slightly. They chatted as usual about the things Felicity wanted to talk about – arguments with her mother, why her father left, the bad behaviour of her mother's current boyfriend. Jasmine couldn't be sure, but she thought she could smell alcohol on Felicity's breath. She knew Felicity liked to drink but it was getting more frequent; she never used to do it at school. As they neared the town Jasmine pulled Felicity into an alcove. She had spotted Tim talking to someone in the entrance to a side street car park a little further down the road.

'What are you doing?' Felicity asked.

'Shhhh, be quiet, I don't want to spook him.'

'Spook who?'

'See that guy over there? He's our new lodger.'

'You didn't tell me he was hot,' Felicity said, trying to get a good look at him.

'Is that all you think about?' Jasmine said.

'Oh, like you haven't thought of it? Do me a favour.' Felicity pulled her red lipstick out of her bag and put it on using the reflection in the glass door as a mirror.

'Can you hear what they're saying?'

'Do you think he would get us some booze if we gave him some money?'

'Shut up, I'm trying to listen.'

Jasmine could hear fragments of the conversation. It wasn't a friendly one. She peeked around the corner and saw Tim's face; he looked intense and focused as his index finger jabbed the other man square in the centre of his chest. The stranger looked afraid.

'I told you, I need that money back by Friday, and it's Tuesday now. What do you suppose I should do with you?' Tim barked.

'Please don't hurt me,' the man was pleading, which surprised Jasmine. It sounded like a request made out of fear. Had Tim hurt this man?

'I did you a favour and now you're letting me down. If you can't get me the money, then you had better consider what it is you *can* get for me. I'll come back tomorrow. Don't disappoint me.'

Tim stepped away and looked in the girls' direction. They ducked back behind the wall. Jasmine's heart was thumping. She looked to see if there was anywhere for them to go. What if he came past them? What if he confronted her? Instead, Jasmine saw him disappear into the side street that led to the car park. The charity shop they were headed for was just a few metres up the road. When the coast was clear Jasmine grabbed Felicity by the arm and pulled her quickly down the street. Once they were safely inside the shop, Felicity started laughing. Jasmine joined in, but in the back of her mind she couldn't help thinking about what she had just witnessed. This wasn't the man that she saw helping out around the house; there was something very sinister about the way he had been talking to that man. What had her parents brought into their home?

Chapter Twelve

Jasmine woke up early, with a couple of hours until her revision class at school. It was just too hot today; the relief from the bit of rain yesterday had been short-lived. She tried to go back to sleep but the heat was frustrating. Her sheets clung to her and she felt the anger building inside as she wrestled against them. She decided to give up and get out of bed. The thought of putting on her school shirt made her feel even hotter; the poor-quality fabric would cut into her armpits and make her sweat more. Her hair was wet at the temples and her face felt clammy to the touch. She could barely breathe and it wasn't even six a.m. A cold shower was the only way she could think of to cool down. She was out in less than five minutes and she pulled out a white T-shirt and some shorts to dress in until the last possible moment before school. The lingering smell of paint inside her bedroom was doing nothing to make her feel refreshed and so she grabbed her Spanish homework and went downstairs.

She cut up a melon from the fridge and went to sit in the garden to eat it. It was early enough that the part of the garden where the sun loungers lived was still in the shade. Yesterday Tim had started painting the facing wall white at her parents' instruction. It had a Mediterranean vibe about it. Jasmine's mother loved geraniums and the bright oranges, reds and pinks looked almost neon against the white backdrop.

The guest house door opened and Tim came outside. He nodded his acknowledgement of Jasmine, glancing at her bare legs but looking away quickly. He pulled a dustsheet off of his painting equipment in the corner of the garden and started to work immediately. Did Jasmine imagine he had been messing with her at the breakfast table? Maybe she just didn't understand social cues. A wave of self-doubt came over her and she thought back to what had happened at school last year. Did she just not have the ability to read other people at all?

Tim continued to paint the wall with almost

complete indifference to her presence. She looked at the clock; she still had a good hour before she had to go to school.

'Do you need any help?' she offered, before she had even really thought about it. She remembered her father telling her to make more of an effort and she had realised that she didn't like being ignored.

'Thank you. Just grab any brush and start painting,' Tim said, pointing to the box of brushes.

She chose one and started at the opposite end of the wall to him. It felt therapeutic to be turning this tired old dirty lemon wall into something fresh and new. The surface was rougher than an inside wall, taking a little more effort, so she began working the paint into the cracks and tiny holes. Tim had already filled in all the bigger ones, but her mother had insisted she didn't want it to look too perfect or it would lose its charm.

As they painted, they got closer together and it wasn't long before they were standing side by side. They had worked together in silence, which, when Jasmine thought about it, was a strange thing to do. Tim's bare arm touched hers as they finally met in the middle.

'Wow, guys, that looks amazing,' Jasmine's father called out across the garden, adding, 'I hope she's not giving you too much trouble.'

'None at all.'

She felt annoyed at her father in that moment for saying such a dismissively 'dad' thing. He knew she was no trouble; he was just saying that for something to say, something he had seen some other dad say, on TV maybe. Frank did things like this sometimes, and she'd heard him repeat other people's opinions and pass them off as his. She wasn't entirely sure her father had any real opinions of his own. Most of the things he said were second hand, something her mother had said before, or something he had seen on TV.

'We're off to work now. Keep an eye on the time, Jasmine.'

Again, his words annoyed her. Treating her like a baby. She heard him go back inside and she relaxed again.

'I had better go. Where should I put this?' she asked Tim. As she looked at him a smile broke out on his face.

'Come here.'

He reached up and slid his hand under her hair; she flinched backwards a little until he cradled her head in his hand. He licked his thumb and placed his other hand on her cheek, sweeping away what she assumed was paint. She felt slightly limp. He gently removed his hand from her neck, and she felt as though she could fall straight backwards. Instead, she went back inside and upstairs.

She peeked out of her bedroom window when she got back to her room. He seemed so completely different to the man she had seen in town threatening that stranger. Maybe the other man had been asking for it – she didn't know the full story. Either way, Tim's behaviour was confusing her; one minute he was sweet and kind and at other times he was almost sinister. Jasmine felt like she had no choice but to keep an eye on him for now. He didn't make any sense.

Chapter Thirteen

Now

I'm so torn between needing to know the truth and being afraid of it that I can barely sleep. Despite being warm in the day there is a wind outside in the night and it whips at the sea. I hear the faintest sound of a tree branch gently thumping against some guttering, almost like a tap on a door. I am standing in the dark looking outside, a small bottle of whisky in my hand, the third and final one from the minibar. I have all the lights off so I can see the outside better and not just my own reflection, my outline against the glass like a ghost. This place is full of ghosts, including me.

The front is empty now, no stragglers or

ramblers, no dog walkers, no bohemian travellers. Just the promenade, the pebble beach and the sea. I remember in the winter how angry the sea used to be. How the town would gather after a heavy storm and fix what the storm had destroyed. In the past, walls had been pulled down, lamp posts felled, hotels flooded, windows broken, and all by water. Unless you witnessed it, it was hard to imagine, the tide coming in, crashing against the concrete jetties. It was a game to stand close to the edge and wait for a wave before we all ran away screaming and laughing, some of us not quite getting away in time to avoid the splash of salty water. I don't think anyone really appreciated how dangerous it was; it was just a way to pass the time, a break in the routine.

Now that I am back here, I find myself remembering good things I hadn't allowed myself to think about for fear of remembering something bad. The moment I walked away I closed a part of me down, like an attic with a rotten floor. No matter what treasures lay inside, I had no desire to investigate and risk losing myself to the past. Finding Chris was what saved me; if I had never met him I don't know who I would be now. I dread to think. His kindness was what pulled me in; I needed it. I still need it. He will be up now; he goes in to work early. I grab my mobile and call him. I hope he has forgiven me for walking away. I half expect him not to answer – just being here makes me wonder if my life away wasn't all just a dream. Maybe I never left at all.

'Flick?' he answers, and I feel tears appear almost immediately. I missed him more than I realised.

'Hey. I just wanted to say hi.'

'How is it going there? Are you OK?' he says, warm as ever and I wonder if I imagined him being annoyed. I know that sometimes my paranoia gets the best of me. It's served me well in the past, though.

'I'm good, it's good to hear your voice.'

'I wasn't sure if you would call,' he said.

'Why wouldn't I? I miss you guys,' I say, sad that I even have to tell him that I miss them.

'You were just acting really strange before you left. I was worried about you.'

'Are you still coming down at the weekend? Would be good to see you.' I feel like I might never see him again. This place has a way of keeping you here. It's hard to get away.

'We will be down as soon as we can. I love you. I have to get in to work now.' I hear a thickness in his voice, as though he is holding back tears.

'I love you, too,' I say, but he has already gone. I hope he knows without hearing me say it.

I straighten my hair and my fringe, line my eyes and add the red lips. I want to be out when the shops are opening, before the town livens up. It's a good opportunity to talk to local people, if I can even get up the nerve. I wear boots today, even though it's warm, because I plan on being out for most of the day and I don't want to give myself any excuse to retreat back to the hotel like a coward.

I walk onto the promenade and along the front. I remember we used to sit in the shelter and shout at passers-by. Entertainment was what you made of it in a place like this. The shelter has had a couple of layers of paint added since I lived here, but it's the same one. I remember when they installed it. I sit on the bench inside and run my fingers along the wooden slats. The first time we got drunk was in this little hut. We sneaked bottles of Vermouth and got one of the older boys in town to buy us cider. We drank the Vermouth straight and in too short a space of time. Afterwards we walked to the cemetery and jumped out at each other from behind gravestones. I still feel bad for throwing up on a grave, even though it was well over a hundred years old and clearly hadn't been visited anytime recently. I had forgotten about that night until just now. I remember getting home and pretending I was sober and my mother playing along, or perhaps she was too blind to reality to notice, even though I could tell she knew I had been drinking.

I look up and down the promenade to check for anyone else, but there is no one apart from the occasional car on the adjacent road and so I lie on the concrete walkway. I have lain here before. I carved our initials in the wood under the bench. I wondered if it was preserved. It was; faded but the same and still recognisably in my handwriting. *F & J forever*. Except nothing lasts forever, not even in this picture-perfect little town.

Chapter Fourteen

I walk along the high street I have walked down a million times before – the same gift shops and charity shops, the same bakeries and clothing shops. I know where to start my search, although I'm still unsure of exactly what I'm looking for, still ignoring the whispers at the back of my mind that are telling me I already know what happened. I don't know why I thought I needed to be here, all I know is that I do. I have to find out what I missed when I ran away. The library is as good a place as any to start.

Something catches my eye as I turn down the little road to go into the library. A car on the mini roundabout just on the edge of the centre. I see the tail end as it twists into the adjacent road; the colour looks like faded mahogany. I know that car. I stop dead for a few moments, scared that I am imagining things. Why would that car be here? Why now? Was I supposed to see it? I turn down the small side road into the library, partly to be off the main street. I feel sick at the thought that I have been discovered already. I enter the library and go to the reference section to look at old copies of the local newspaper, *The Echo*, to look for names, faces and stories about all the people I have tried to forget, all the people I left behind. I need to figure out who to speak to about the missing girl. In the back of my mind I keep seeing the car disappearing around the corner; did that really happen or am I just seeing an apparition of the past? This place is already playing tricks on me.

I remember the headlines when she disappeared. I remember being grateful it wasn't me and then feeling guilty for that. I go to the archive and look for the dates; now that I am here I am ready to start making my way down the rabbit hole. I am embarrassed that I don't remember the exact dates – I should remember, shouldn't I? That summer changed my life. That was the summer I met him, that was the summer I realised you couldn't even trust your best friend not to stab you in the back. That whole summer was a lesson in why you should never trust anyone. People lie and twist things to suit their own agenda; people manipulate you to get what they want. Even the people who say they love you more than anything in the world.

I find the paper describing the girl that went missing at the fair. I remember her face that night as she stood under the Ferris wheel, her hair changing colour as the lights reflected off it. There are moments in your life that you wish you could go back to and make different decisions. I wish I could go back to that fair and tell that girl to be careful, tell her not to get in any cars or talk to any strangers. I think about my Daisy and how when you're young you just never think it's going to be you. Bad things only happen to other people, never to you, never to the people you love. Until you learn that lesson the hard way. It can happen to anyone, at any time. You can be good or bad, it doesn't matter, it's all random, there is no higher power, no reward or punishment system. Bad things happen to good people all the time and bad people often prosper in life.

I look at the newspapers after the date of her disappearance, to see if there is any more information. She was an only child, her parents were completely devastated, and as I move through the archive I see that occasionally they've taken out adverts in the paper appealing for information;

to this day they are still trying to find out what happened to their daughter. I push it to the back of my mind. I can't be sure that I know what happened to her. All I have are suspicions, all I have are theories I can't get the answers to. I thought I knew the truth once. I was horribly wrong.

There were several suspects in her disappearance, although only one person got lumbered with the blame and to this day I still don't know if he did it. He already had a terrible reputation and everyone was happy to have a face to put to the crime, so they accepted his guilt with ease. Knowing what I know now, I just don't think it was that simple. I think we were all to blame. We all looked the other way because it suited our narrative of what 'bad' looks like. I know now that you can't take anyone at face value, that you should never just accept the version of a person they put in front of you. The nicer someone is, the more you have to fear.

Chapter Fifteen

Then

Jasmine and Felicity walked down towards the town together, having waited until eight to venture out, hoping all the smaller children would be gone from the fair already. It was still warm even though the light was turning, the twilight sky a furious pink as they approached the park. They might even make it to the fair in time to watch the sun sink into the sea, those last angry stripes lingering in the sky as it disappeared. It was better at the fair in the dark; it felt like more of an experience, more value for money. Frank had given Jasmine thirty quid to spend but she wasn't great with heights so there were only a few rides that she would go on. Once Jasmine had tried the Ferris wheel, which wasn't even a big one, but she'd freaked out and screamed until they let her off. It was the way the seat swung, making her think she might fall out of the back. Her dad hated fairground rides – he had never told Jasmine why – and so when she was little it was only ever her mum who brought her. Even though the fair came to town every year, Jasmine rarely saw the same workers twice, which seemed strange to her as the rides were always the same and it was always the same company. She wondered what happened to the people who left the fair.

As Jasmine and Felicity walked through the Byes, a park that ran along the river from Sidford right down to the town, they were hit with the smell of marijuana. Jasmine looked over to the willow tree that hung like curtains over the riverbank. Jason Evans and Hannah Torrence were underneath it smoking a credit-card-shaped hash pipe, trying to be inconspicuous but failing miserably as they both giggled uncontrollably, clearly stoned.

Jasmine tried not to stare as they passed them, noting she had never seen either of them smile before, both perpetually uncomfortable people who had black painted fingernails and long black woollen coats, even in this weather. Jasmine and

Felicity exited the park and crossed the street to the ford crossing, a small road for cars to cross to get to the car park over the river without going through the town centre. Jasmine used to get so excited by it as a child, convinced they were driving through very deep water, but now that she was older she could see that it was only a few inches and never warranted the anticipation she had given it. Jasmine could see others from their class heading across the little bridge over the water. Not willing to make any rash decisions about who to hang with just yet, they all pretended they hadn't seen each other and carried on.

Jasmine was particularly struck by what a closed little community her classmates were whenever she came back from her family's travels abroad – like a tiny cosmos that always stayed the same, a secret hidden in the valley. She noticed the sideways glances towards anyone who didn't fit in, who wasn't part of the accepted genetic make-up of the locals. Jasmine knew people who had never even taken a bus out of town; their world began and ended there. Felicity was one of those people. Aside from visiting her uncle in Spain once, Felicity had never left the confines of the town. Felicity's relationship with her mother was fractious and the more time the two girls spent together the more grateful Jasmine was for her own family situation. Felicity's mother Carol spent most of her money on drink and cigarettes so they didn't really do family holidays and Flick hadn't seen her biological father in over five years, even though he lived less than half an hour away. They didn't talk about it much, but it was clear to Jasmine that Felicity had inherited her mother's taste for alcohol and sometimes when she was drunk she would say things, enough that Jasmine could see why Felicity was so desperate to get so far away from the town and her mother. Jasmine couldn't imagine that.

Jasmine also wondered how her own parents had come to settle in this pretty little part of the world. Both Frank and Lisa loved to travel, always had, and they loved all different kinds of people and cultures, yet there they were in the most English and insular of towns, tucked away in its own little microcosm. Being there seemed the opposite of who they were. Her parents weren't from the area, although they never really discussed much from before they met, and so she wasn't entirely sure where her father was from originally. Jasmine's mother was less secretive and sometimes told her about her life on a farm, although she was sure she remembered Lisa once telling her that the farm was in Hertfordshire and another time that it was in Wiltshire. Jasmine had learned not to ask – Frank had always maintained it wasn't where you come from but who you are that matters.

'Maybe we can find someone for you,' Felicity said.

'Not interested. Please don't try and set me up with anyone.'

'What if Taylor is there?' Felicity said.

'You know full well he will be there, everyone's going to be there.'

'You don't fancy him at all?'

'No, I don't think so. I don't fancy anyone at school.'

'Maybe you will fancy one of the Carneys.'

'I'm really not that bothered about getting off with anyone to be honest, Flick, that's more your thing.'

'Are you calling me a tramp?' Flick said with feigned offence. Jasmine just raised her eyebrows and broke out into a sprint before Felicity had a chance to wallop her.

They were almost at the fair and she felt the butterflies in her stomach, feelings of chaos and possibility mingling together. That's why the fair was so exciting. Jasmine knew Felicity was wondering if the guy she lost her V to would be there. In a way, Jasmine hoped he was; she wanted to see how they would react to each other. She suspected he wasn't how Felicity remembered him.

Before they reached the fair, Felicity pulled a small bottle of Mad Dog out of her satchel; it was bright green and looked like nuclear waste.

'Come on, let's have this before we go in.'

'Where did you get that?'

'My mum's current boytoy bought a couple of boxes of them. They're all out of date but I'm not sure how good this stuff is for you even when it's in date.'

'Won't he miss them?'

'I don't care if he does. What's he going to do about it? Tell Mum? I doubt it.'

'What even is it?' Jasmine said.

Felicity opened the bottle and took a long swig before handing it to Jasmine.

'Don't know but it does the job, right?'

She took a drink before handing it back to Flick, who drank another few gulps before giving the remainder to Jasmine, who tossed it in the public bin when she was done. It wasn't about the flavour or quality, it was just about drinking, rebelling, being a different version of yourself.

The first thing they went on was the dodgems, an easy way into the rides and an equal playing field. They could ram their car into whoever they wanted to; there was no social pyramid on the dodgem court. Jasmine's stomach lurched as she saw Taylor Hines in the queue waiting for one to become available. She knew he hadn't seen her yet. She'd kissed Taylor at the school disco last year to prove a point, but it had been a great source of embarrassment for both of them ever since. She could see Felicity getting ready to ram his car as soon as he chose one. They weren't so different, she and Felicity, they both had a morbid but friendly fascination with seeing each other in really uncomfortable situations, especially with boys.

'Let's go on something else,' Jasmine pleaded as they watched him get into the bright pink dodgem.

'Not a chance. Let's ram him.'

'You're not supposed to, we'll get told off.'

'They're called bumper cars, you're meant to bump people. And I want to bump Taylor.'

Secretly Jasmine kind of wanted to bump his car as well. They had both avoided each other like the plague since the kiss but she did like seeing him squirm. There wasn't a hierarchy as such in their social group, but if there was, she would be a few rungs down on the ladder from Taylor; he was definitely one of the more popular kids. Jasmine moving to Carlton Road had shifted her up the ladder a bit, but Taylor lived on Laskey's Lane in a very expensive house overlooking the sea.

Felicity rammed their car straight into Taylor, who looked up, startled. They had him pinned against the wall and he was desperately trying to avoid making eye contact with Jasmine, which of course Felicity found hilarious. Jasmine felt powerful, knowing that he couldn't get away no matter how much he wanted to. But then she looked beyond Taylor and saw Tim.

He was talking with one of the fairground guys in the shadows between a couple of the caravans. She knew it was Tim because he had a way of standing that was so distinctive and different that it just couldn't be anyone else. It was as though he was leaning against an invisible wall, his head tilted down so that he was always looking up at you. She tried to keep her eyes on him and work out what he was doing. Felicity spun the dodgem around and then when Jasmine looked back to the darkened corner, it was empty. He was gone. She looked around the fairground but she couldn't see him anywhere. Maybe she hadn't seen him at all.

They got off the dodgems and Jasmine spotted Jason again, the boy from their class they had seen in the Byes, standing nearby. He was quiet and a bit of a loner, apart from when he was with one of the other loners, like Hannah. Jasmine got the impression that he was normally alone out of choice and not because no one liked him – it was more as if he had a low tolerance for other people. He was always pleasant enough, but you could see his eyes darting around as he looked for an escape. Jason was a bit of a mystery, but that suited him. He was kind of cool in his own way; there were rumours that his older brother was a pot dealer and that was why he almost got a pass from a lot of the other kids, even though he was strange and that wasn't usually allowed. Jasmine watched Jason and Hannah walk away from the fair, towards the path that ran along the side of the stream. No doubt to snog or smoke pot again, or both.

'What next? Should we do the waltzers or the anti-grav?' Felicity asked, pulling Jasmine's attention away from Jason and Hannah. The last time they did the anti-grav Jasmine threw up, but it was Felicity's favourite ride so Jasmine shrugged.

'I need the loo. You go get in the queue for the anti-grav and I'll meet you over there in a bit,' Jasmine said, walking off before Felicity had a chance to argue. She saw her go and stand next to Taylor in the queue; they were close, chatting. Jasmine suspected that Felicity liked him and that was why she made a point of trying to embarrass her in front of him all the time. Jasmine could tell Felicity was relieved to be alone with him, glad that Jasmine was gone.

The Port Royal toilets were outside of the park and towards the sea, next to the sailing club. Jasmine walked away from the fair alone, everywhere else dark as the beach was poorly lit. The sea was completely black, the moon hidden behind the only cloud in the sky. She started to feel uncomfortable as she got closer to the public toilets, thinking she should have made Felicity go with her.

'Jasmine.'

She turned to see Mr Morrell coming across the bridge from the clifftop path that was hidden out of view from the fair. She instantly felt a little sick. Why was he there? Had he been waiting on the off chance that she would turn up? She didn't want to talk to him but she didn't know what she was supposed to do. There was no point calling out, no one would hear her over the noise of the fair. She edged backwards towards the toilets but, all things considered, she thought she was safer out in the open.

'What do you want?' she said, feeling strange not calling him by his name. Disrespectful, somehow.

'I just wanted to explain things to you,' he said, sounding panicked, upset.

'You explained in your letter. I'm not supposed to talk to you. You're definitely not supposed to talk to me.'

'I couldn't say everything I needed to in that letter. I knew other people would read it.'

'I need to get back to the fair. I can't talk to you. What would your fiancée think if you get caught talking to me again?'

'Please, just talk to me.' He was close to her now. He looked different now that he was no longer her teacher. He looked younger and definitely more pathetic. He was wearing jeans and a T-shirt, whereas at school he had always worn a waistcoat and looked very put together. Not any more.

'Just leave me alone.' She went to walk away and he grabbed her arm. His fingers dug into her flesh and she knew there was no way she could shake herself free. Her anxiety increased as she imagined him dragging her onto the beach or into the toilets, both of which were close enough that he could take her there with ease, without anyone noticing.

'I thought we had something, I thought you wanted me to kiss you.'

'Well, I didn't,' she snapped. She felt his grip tighten and worried that she had made things worse. 'You were my teacher, you are engaged to be married, I didn't think of you like that at all. I'm sorry you thought I did.'

He pulled her towards him. Panicked, Jasmine

looked towards the fair and saw someone walking through the path between the hedges from the swimming pool car park.

'Help!' she shouted, but Morrell's hand covered her mouth before she could shout again.

'I'm not going to hurt you. I just want you to admit that you wanted me to kiss you. You ruined my life and it wasn't just in my mind, you wanted me, Jazz, admit it!' His eyes were brimming with desperation and she knew she had to calm things down. She hoped Felicity would come to look for her soon, although she doubted that she would as she was talking to Taylor.

'Jasmine. Are you all right?' she heard from behind her. She couldn't see him but she knew it was Tim; she recognised his voice. Morrell relaxed his grip and confusion swept across his face, whatever emotion he was in the grips of seemingly vanishing as soon as someone else was around.

'Who are you?' Mr Morrell's gaze snapped away from Jasmine to look directly behind her. He let go and Jasmine staggered backwards until her arm thumped against Tim. She hadn't even noticed that she was crying until she was a few feet away from Mr Morrell.

'I'm a friend of Jasmine's. Who are you?' She felt Tim's hand on her shoulder. It steadied her. She was shaking.

Mr Morrell didn't respond.

Jasmine could see Mr Morrell trying to work out her connection to Tim, his gaze locked on the hand that rested on her shoulder. She saw a flash of jealousy and then anger. She felt safe with Tim next to her. Before now she hadn't been sure of Tim but the threat of being alone with Mr Morrell put those childish feelings in perspective. The men stared at each other and Jasmine stepped to the side so she could watch them both. Tim had his eyes fixed on Mr Morrell, a slight smile on his face. There was something menacing about it and yet she still felt safe, glad she was on the right side of his expression.

'I think you should go,' Tim said. 'Unless you want to try and grab me. I guarantee you won't do nearly as well against someone the same size as you – well, bigger.'

Mr Morrell just backed away. She could see that he still wanted to talk, but not with Tim here. Jasmine knew he was considering his chances of winning a fight but then he clearly thought better of it and broke into a run back across the bridge and up the path that led to the houses at the top of the cliff. He lived in one of them – Jasmine knew because during one of their chats he'd told her his bedroom overlooked the sea. At the time she thought it was a strange thing to tell her, but now she knew he had the wrong idea about them it made sense. There was a restraining order in place and he couldn't be within a hundred metres of Jasmine. As she thought about the look on his face she wondered if the restraining order made a difference at all; would he violate it again or had Tim scared him off for good?

She stared with bated breath across the bridge until she was sure Mr Morrell was gone. Then Jasmine rushed forwards and clutched Tim. He put his arms around her to comfort her.

'Oh my God, thank you. I don't know what I would have done if you hadn't turned up.'

'Who was that?' he asked, letting go of her. She stepped back and suddenly felt very awkward about the fact that she just had her arms wrapped around his waist.

'It's a long story. He's no one, really. He's harmless.'

'You seem scared of him,' Tim said softly, as though he were trying to coax information from her, or maybe she just wanted to tell him.

'My parents didn't tell you the story? They told everyone else.'

'They haven't told me anything.'

'He was a teacher at my school. He lost his job because of some stuff he did.'

Tim shifted his gaze to the path. 'What's up there?'

'Houses. He lives in one of them. I think so, anyway.'

'What do you mean by "stuff"?'

'It was nothing, he just got confused about me and then kissed me. He didn't know there was a camera in the library and when the school found out he got into loads of trouble and lost his job,' Jasmine blurted out, unsure why she sounded apologetic.

'Did you kiss him back?'

'What? No.'

'Is that all he did?'

'I was on library duty at school and we were talking. I can't even remember exactly what we were talking about; he talked to me a lot. I thought it was just because he knew I loved reading and books. Anyway, he pushed me up against the shelves and kissed me. Apparently he grabbed me as well but I don't remember that part. The cameras got everything, he got caught, lost his job, case closed.'

'Grabbed you?'

'Just . . . you know . . .' She gestured towards her chest, not wanting to say the words, not sure which words to use. She saw a flicker of anger in his face just before he turned his head towards the clifftop path and looked intently for a few moments.

'I should get back to the fair. My friend Felicity is waiting for me,' she said. She was starting to feel uneasy again.

She was alone in the dark with Tim. She saw a shift in him, too, also uncomfortable at the situation. He paused for a moment.

'Why don't I take you home instead? You should tell your parents.'

'Please don't tell them, they'll just ask me a million questions and put me in counselling again.'

'Let's just get you home safe. He might come back.'

'Fine. I'll just text Felicity and let her know I'm leaving.'

She pulled out her phone and told Felicity that she didn't feel well and her dad had picked her up. She didn't know why she was lying to her friend, but she just couldn't face the teasing or questions. Mr Morrell did scare her a little. He hadn't before, but this incident was different. She had misunderstood the extent of his feelings; it didn't seem like he was going to let it go. He was absolutely convinced that she felt the same way about him and that other people were keeping them apart. She didn't know what would have happened if Tim hadn't been there tonight. Mr Morrell could have dragged her into any of those dark little corners of the beach; she got

110

chills just thinking about it. Everyone was so focused on the fair that she doubted they would have noticed; with so many screams coming from the rides, any screaming she might have done wouldn't even register.

'Are you OK? You're shivering,' Tim said.

'I don't know what I would have done if you hadn't been here. Thank you.'

'It's OK. I'm glad I was here, too.' He smiled softly. 'He's not going to come near you again, OK?'

She followed Tim to his car, occasionally looking behind her to check that Mr Morrell was really gone. As they pulled away, Jasmine saw that her hands were shaking, her fingers cold despite the never-ending heatwave.

She hoped that was the last she ever saw of Mr Morrell.

Chapter Sixteen

Now

I have printed off several articles at the library. Anything mentioning the girl's name, anything mentioning any suspects at the time, wondering whose name I might see there. I didn't read the papers back then, I just saw them lying around in waiting rooms, or walked past them in the shops. Rumours are more exciting at that age. It occurs to me how much everything has changed. I pay the librarian for the prints and she looks at me suspiciously as she wrestles the thick stack from the printer tray and hands them over, glancing at the first page.

'I remember this case. Why are you looking at that?'

'I used to know her. I was the same age as her when she went missing. It was a dreadful shock at the time. This other girl going missing has brought everything back and I just wanted to read about her again,' I say, overcome with guilt over the past, feeling bad for opening the cupboards and pulling out the skeletons.

'Terrible business. You just don't expect that kind of thing around here. I just can't believe it's happened again. Why anyone would copy that monster.'

'What makes you think it was a copy?' I ask.

'Well, it's just so similar, isn't it? The girl was last seen at the bus stop – funny, I never thought about that before. But they got the guy who did it last time, didn't they? So someone must have copied him . . .'

She rambled on but I had stopped listening. *Did* they get the right man last time? We were all so sure when it happened, but I'm not so sure now. I don't think any of us really knew what was happening right under our noses. That's what happens in a place like this. People buy into the image of perfection and everyone is willing to look the other way to maintain it. Once someone is persona non grata then they become an easy person to scapegoat. Now that I think about it, maybe that's what happened back then.

'Yes, I guess it is very similar,' I say, as though I hadn't noticed the similarities of the actual case.

'What was her name again? The one that went missing back then?'

'Hannah Torrence.'

'That's the one. Awful thing that was.'

There were only two people in the frame for the disappearance of Hannah Torrence: a teacher at the school, James Morrell, and one of my classmates, Jason Evans. I remember both of them; I suspected both of them. When something like that happens in your town it makes you question everything you know, everyone you know. You wonder if you can ever really know people at all. So many secrets, so many lies.

I want to go back to the hotel and hide, but the day has only just started and I'll never get anywhere if I don't face the past. I left not long after Hannah disappeared. I had nothing left to keep me here when that summer ended. I lost everything and everyone I cared about.

Instead of going back to the hotel, I decide to go to a pub and read through the articles there. Not that I want to get drunk, but I definitely need something to take the edge off my nerves. At home I might go for a run alongside the thickets by the lake, but here I don't much feel like it; I don't want anyone to notice me and so I would rather hide in a corner with some liquid courage. I don't drink this much at home; I think it's being here, in this place. I'm going back in time, becoming the person I used to be, a teenage girl who drank too much and managed to get herself into trouble without even trying. It's strange how being around certain people or being in certain places can change who you are. When I'm with Chris I am weaker somehow, as though I allow him to be the driven one, the brave one, the one who knows things. I bake cakes and make jewellery, I'm on the Parents, Teachers and Friends Association and my children go to every after-school club going. They do gymnastics, ballet, drama club, chess club, horse-back riding and a plethora of other things I can't even remember. I do yoga, I run and I'm in a book club. I have become a housewife by numbers. I focus on making life comfortable for everyone else. It's not as though it feels like a sacrifice, but now I am here it seems strange that this is the woman I became. I remember what I used to want for myself when I am here. I did none of it though. I ran away and almost straight into Chris's arms. It's not his fault either; he never asked me to be this person. I just tried to be normal. I saw how other mothers behaved and copied them. It's all just another disguise, another way of pretending the past didn't happen.

In the pub I read through the stories about Hannah Torrence. See the sensationalist headlines ebb and fade until some other local scandal took its place. It was a long time before they really let it go, though. Memorials and vigils were held, the same faces at every one, the same people interviewed in every article until it was eventually all repeated and regurgitated information.

I am on my fifth vodka and soda when I finally finish reading through all of the papers. There is nothing new there, except at one point they mention the fact that Jason Evans' parents owned a bike shop. Knowing how many people make it out of here, I feel confident that his parents still have the shop, and that Jason is probably still around. I make my next drink a Coke and order myself a lasagne from the lunch menu to try and soak up some of the drink I have had already. Maybe Jason can tell me something the papers didn't know. He's one of the few people connected to the old case that might know something he'd never shared. Might have seen something. Maybe he would open up to me.

As soon as I'm finished with my lunch I leave the pub and walk towards the bike shop. Until now I have been avoiding speaking to anyone I knew, for fear of what they might remember about me, what they might remember about that summer.

Maybe the world didn't fall apart for them in the same way it did for me, but that summer was different. We could all feel it in the air at the time. Maybe it was the heat, or maybe it was something else.

Chapter Seventeen

As I suspected, the bike shop is still there, even though the last mention of it in the newspaper was seven years ago, as far as I could see. The place isn't how I remember it. It was always a dingy, slightly creepy-looking shop. Jason's parents were much older than most other people's and he had an older brother who sold pot who I read in the papers had died in a drink-driving accident up on the back road into town. People used to steer clear of the bike shop for those reasons, and a few more. They were a strange family and if there's one thing people don't like around here, it's anything that ruins the image. The bike shop looked good now, fresh paint on the outside, very slick on the inside with expensive gear mounted on the walls. I take a deep breath before pushing the door open and going inside, a little bell over the entrance announcing my presence.

A man appears from the back of the shop. I can see instantly that it's Jason and I catch my breath.

'Can I help you?'

'Are you Jason Evans?' I ask as I get closer. I can see that he is stoned and I can smell the faintest aroma of marijuana coming off his clothes. He was obviously out back smoking when I came into the shop.

'Who's asking?' he asks cautiously.

'I wanted to ask you some questions about the disappearance of Hannah Torrence.'

'Are you police?' he accuses, anger streaking across his face as soon as I mention Hannah's name.

'No, nothing like that. I just wanted to talk to someone who knew her.'

'Are you from the paper? Because I don't know anything about that new girl that went missing.'

'No, honestly, it's not like that. I knew Hannah a bit, too.'

'What was her favourite band?'

'Green Day,' I say, remembering the most recent photo from the newspaper, where she was wearing the band's hoodie.

'Did you know me? Because me and Hannah were pretty tight back then,' he said, somewhat satisfied with my answer.

'I did, a little. She used to talk about you a lot. My name's Felicity.' I lie, I'd never had a conversation with Hannah about Jason but I thought this might encourage him to speak to me.

'Felicity? You were in my year, right? Your hair is still exactly the same. Wow. How are you? Where have you been?' he says, sizing me up, the faintest look of recognition on his face, but not really; I can see him struggling to place me completely, trying to remember any interactions we may have had. I realise this won't be as difficult as I thought it would although I do feel bad for lying to him about my friendship with Hannah.

'Moved up north, to The Lake District, got married, had a couple of kids. I'm great really.' I smile nervously, depressed that I can boil my entire life down into one short sentence.

'So why are you here, if you live in The Lake District?'

'I heard about the girl going missing on the news and I just had to come down. I wondered if it might be connected in some way. I don't know. I just felt like I had to be here,' I say in a rare moment of honesty.

'I know. It's crazy, isn't it. This week has been

121

a bit triggering to say the least. Can't help thinking back to that night, to what I could have done differently.'

'Did you know her? The girl who just went missing?'

'No, thank God, or they might try to pin that one on me as well. Her name was a bit familiar but then all names are a bit familiar round here aren't they?'

I don't know if it's the alcohol or what, but his comment makes me blurt out a laugh. He smiles and he really is adorable. I should have done this sober; I'm terrified I'll say the wrong thing.

'Why didn't we ever really speak at school?' I ask.

'I don't know. You were one of them girls I just didn't speak to at school, all cool and confident, a bit too good for the rest of us, you know? I mostly mixed with people who scored weed off my brother at the time. You weren't the weed-smoking type. I couldn't wait to get out of there. Had big plans for myself, I did. I wanted to go to art college, become a famous artist and set the world on fire.'

I blush at his description of who he thought I was at the time. So strange to think I was in any way perceived as having an image of confidence and fearlessness when inside I didn't even know who I was yet. If only we could have all seen inside each other, we would have seen we weren't that different after all. He's a good-looking man but he's tarnished with the whispers of the past. Being here kept him as that stoner teenager, stopped him from moving on. He stares at the wall, whether from all the talk of the past or thoughts of a future he never quite reached.

'What happened?'

'My dad had a stroke and they needed me in the shop. Plus, art college was bullshit.'

'And here you are.'

'And here *you* are. Do you remember that party at Cameron Davies' house?' he asks.

'Not really. I don't remember that much to be honest.' I really don't.

'We played spin the bottle and we had to kiss. That's still on my highlight reel from year eleven. You were pretty wasted though. I'd probably get in trouble for that too, these days.'

I wonder if he can tell I have been drinking now. I really need to sober up. This was a bad idea.

'I guess I must have been. I'm sorry.'

'Isn't it weird how something that can mean so much to one person can mean nothing to someone else? The exact same incident. When you kissed me during spin the bottle I didn't even want to wash for a month afterwards.'

'Grim.' I laugh.

'You know what I mean though. With all the popular boys sniffing around you all the time I'm surprised I was lucky enough to even be considered. I remember you didn't even flinch, you just did it. It was sweet, made me feel like a bit less of a loser.' He smiles, blushing.

'It was just a silly game.'

'Not for some of us. It meant something to some of us.' He shrugs.

I feel bad for being so dismissive.

'If it's any consolation, I wish I could remember it.' I realise too late that it sounds like I am flirting and change the subject promptly 'So – Hannah. What happened that night? We saw you together and then she was gone.' I feel like a bitch for not being able to share the moment with him. What I do remember from that night at the Davies house was me hunched over a toilet after drinking a weird spirit from his dad's cabinet that had flecks of gold in it.

'We went to sit on a bench by that little hut, you know, the stone one next to the park by the fair with water filters or something inside it. We went there for a puff on some weed. I tried to kiss Hannah and she got angry. She stormed off and I never saw her again.' He says it robotically, rehearsed and practised as though he has said it a hundred times before – no doubt during all the conversations he had with the police at the time.

'Where did she go?'

'She told me she was going to get the bus home.'

'That was it?'

'I told the police as much. Her parents said it was definitely me. Luckily that other girl came forward about that teacher. What was her name?'

'Jasmine, Jasmine Burgess,' I say, the name sticking to the roof of my mouth, I haven't said it in over fifteen years. It's been buried with all the other things I dare not utter.

'You used to hang around with her, didn't you? Are you still friends?'

'We lost touch. You know how it is.'

'Well, if it hadn't been for all that weird shit that happened between her and that teacher, I don't know what would have happened to me. Hannah's parents were gunning for me pretty hard. They never liked me because I used to wear black nail polish and listen to Green Day; I think they thought I was a Satan worshipper who had sacrificed their daughter in some kind of pagan ritual. Everyone thought I was this weird little loner at school so people were more than happy to think the worst at the first opportunity. Then the police found her wallet in that teacher's car and that was that. Didn't get so much as an apology.'

I have decided that despite not really knowing Jason back then, I like him. I wish I had known him better. I wish maybe something had happened between us, then maybe we could have both been normal. I feel like maybe it was my job to protect him in some way, like I am the only one that could have. If only I hadn't been so blind. He's another casualty of this invisible war that no one even knows is going on.

'Well, I'm sorry to have brought back bad memories. I won't take up any more of your time. Don't want to get you in trouble.'

'Oh God no, I am now in fact actually a weird little loner. Both my parents passed away a few years ago.'

'I'm sorry to hear that.'

'On the upside, it does mean I'm my own boss. I spend most of my days smoking weed and playing PlayStation in the back room. No one's going to come in here today. We could go for a walk and talk more about this, if you want?'

I look over at him for a moment, that sweet underused smile on his face. 'I'd like that.'

'Give me five minutes to lock up.'

I feel like I'm cheating on Chris even though all I've done is ask a few questions. But Jason is undeniably attractive and he has a way about him, a confidence. I remember it a little from the way he didn't succumb to any kind of peer pressure back then. If only we were all that wise.

He locks up the shop and comes outside. We walk back down the road towards the centre and Jason lights up a cigarette before offering me one, which I decline.

'I can't believe it's happened again. When I saw on the news that a girl had gone missing I was half expecting to be arrested immediately.'

'I'm sorry.'

'Did you think I did it? Back then I mean.'

'No. I never thought you did it.'

'That's something, I suppose. Took me a long time to get over it. Felt like everyone was looking at me all the time, judging me and stuff. The police questioned me relentlessly for twenty-four hours, it was horrible.'

'Must have been hard.'

'Not as hard as whatever happened to Hannah,' he says, and I hear his voice crack a little. I guess it never occurred to me how hard that year might have been for him, for anyone really. I have always been so wrapped up in my own drama, it's something I truly hate about myself.

'Did they ever find her?' I ask, knowing the answer already, unsure why I am asking.

'No. They never did.'

Chapter Eighteen

Then

Jasmine ate cereal in the kitchen with the radio on, as Tim worked on redecorating the pantry, a tiny room off the kitchen that was lined with the most offensive wallpaper Jasmine had ever seen. The skit on the radio was some awful schlocky prank call show where the presenter phoned a random local business and tried to get the owner to say a specific word without letting them in on the joke and, if they did, the show would give five hundred quid to charity. Today the word was 'penetrate'. Jasmine cringed just listening to it. The segment finished and the news came on, with an appeal for a missing girl, last seen at the local bus depot a little after nine. Hannah Torrence.

Jasmine felt her stomach drop. She had been standing next to her just the day before, at the fair.

Tim came out of the pantry and looked around to check Jasmine's parents weren't there. 'Did you tell them about last night yet?'

'No.'

'You hear that on the radio? A girl went missing. You have to tell them.'

'I don't think he would do anything like that. Maybe she just ran away,' she said, unconvinced by her own words.

'He wasn't well, that man. He was dangerous. What would have happened if I hadn't been there? That could have been you on the news,' Tim said.

Tim was right. A strange mixture of relief and guilt washed over her. Had she led Mr Morrell on? Had she turned him into the person who grabbed hold of her? Did he come back down from the clifftop and take his anger out on someone else? On Hannah? She remembered how Tim had come out of nowhere and rescued her. He had been so protective.

'My parents will never let me out of the house again if I tell them this. I'll be grounded for ever, lo-jacked probably, and forced into some kind of home-schooling situation in a windowless room. You have no idea how they reacted last time. Everyone will hate me – they hated me last time, said it was my fault that he did what he did. He might not have anything to do with what happened last night and the police won't look for anyone else if I just drop him in it – and how will Hannah's family feel if they think he was coming after me instead?'

'None of that matters. Justice is what matters. You don't have to tell them anything beyond what actually happened. This might come out eventually and then where will you be? How will people feel about you then? You can't keep this to yourself, it's not your secret to keep. What if he took that girl?' Tim was more invested than Jasmine expected him to be; he seemed genuinely upset at the disappearance of this girl. She had to ask herself why he was so desperate for her to put Mr Morrell in the frame. He was right about one thing though, the truth always came out, and so she really felt like she had no choice.

The stairs creaked, alerting Jasmine that Lisa was coming down. She jumped up and put the kettle on before her mother arrived in the room.

'OK, I'll tell her,' Jasmine whispered over the sound of the kettle.

'Do you want me to go?'

'No, stay.' Jasmine wanted to gauge his reaction as she told her mother.

Jasmine pulled a mug out of the cupboard and started to make her mother a coffee, to give her something to focus on while she was telling Lisa about what had happened at the fair.

'Morning, Jazz. Ooh, could you make me one?'

'This one's for you,' Jasmine said. She looked over at the pantry to where Tim was leaning against the door with his arms folded, as if he were just part of the scenery.

'Oh, I thought it might be for Tim.'

'I'm fine, I just had one,' he said, before turning his head to Jasmine and nodding ever so slightly.

'I need to talk to you about something,' Jasmine said. No point delaying it now.

'What is it?' Lisa asked, seeming almost excited at the prospect of a rare heart-to-heart with her daughter, especially one she didn't have to insti-gate. Jasmine put the coffee in front of her mother on the dining table, before sliding into the chair opposite her. She wished she had a mug to hold onto; she didn't know what to do with her hands.

'I saw Mr Morrell last night.'

'What? Where?' Lisa's eyes widened with alarm,

'At the fair,' Jasmine said.

'He was at the fair? He's not supposed to be around kids,' Lisa said, her nostrils flared and lips pursed together in a tight knot, her jaw twitching as she tried to suppress her anger.

'He wasn't at the fair. I went to the loo and he came up to me.'

'He was in the toilets?' Lisa said, horrified, her voice jumping several octaves.

'No. Mum, calm down, it was on the way to the loos on the front.'

'Were you alone?' she asked, a little calmer, obviously trying not to spook Jasmine into shutting down.

'Yes, Flick was in the queue for one of the rides – it was huge and so I just said I would go and come back rather than us both losing our spot.'

'What did he do? Did he hurt you?'

'No, nothing like that.'

'Then what?'

'He just said he wanted to talk, he grabbed my arm and he was crying, it was all really weird.'

'That fucking snake. Wait 'til I tell your father; he's going to go ballistic,' Lisa said through her teeth.

'It's fine, I don't think he will bother me again,' Jasmine said, mostly to convince herself. He hadn't got the message and it was clear he had no intention of giving up – she had been able to tell that much from those few terrifying moments with him.

'And he just let you go? He didn't do anything . . . sexual?'

'Mum!'

'You know what I mean, Jazz.'

Jasmine looked over towards Tim, still standing quietly with his arms folded. 'Tim was there, he stopped him. I think he scared the shit out of him. Mr Morrell ran off and Tim brought me home.'

'Why the hell didn't you tell us?' Lisa snapped at Tim angrily.

'I begged him not to. He told me I should tell you guys. I was just afraid you would lose it completely,' Jasmine said. Tim didn't seem particularly bothered by Lisa's outburst as he maintained his same casual stance in the doorway.

'I'm sorry, Mrs B, I just didn't want to break Jasmine's trust like that. She was pretty upset at the time and I didn't want to make things worse.'

'So you broke our trust instead?' Lisa said. It was the first time Jasmine had seen her annoyed with Tim.

'Don't be mad at him. If he hadn't been there, I don't know what would have happened. I just heard on the news that a girl went missing after the fair. You don't think it was Mr Morrell, do you?'

'We'll have to speak to the police,' Lisa said, her demeanour suddenly calmer, as if she had somehow accepted the situation was resolved. 'Is there anything else you haven't told me?'

'No, that's it. I swear.'

'I had better call your dad to come back for when you speak to the police. You shouldn't be keeping secrets from us, Jasmine.'

'I just didn't want you to freak out like last year,' Jasmine said, although that was only part of it; the other part was that she didn't want to be this eternal victim, she just wanted to be normal and like all the other girls in her year without her parents hawking over her every move and making her feel like somehow this was all her fault. Whether or not that had ever been their intention, it was how they made her feel, and she was the one who had to adjust her behaviour after the incident at school. It had all felt like a punishment.

'I think you should write down what you remember from last night. I'm going to grab a shower and then we will call the police when your father comes home,' Lisa said, seeming exasperated.

The legal proceedings against Mr Morrell had been very public and exhausting, with some people more than convinced that Jasmine was lying just to ruin a good man's career, despite the fact that there was video evidence and it wasn't Jasmine who was pushing the case forward, it was her parents. The thought of going through all that again was less than appealing and Jasmine knew that if it wasn't for this missing girl and some form of civic duty, her parents would probably want to keep the police out of it. As much good will as they had within the community, it would always be hard to be a talking point in a small town like this.

Her mother left her coffee on the table and disappeared upstairs. Jasmine grabbed a pen and paper from the kitchen drawer.

'I saw you at the fair,' she said to Tim. 'You were arguing with one of the blokes who worked there. I thought I was imagining it, until you found me talking to Mr Morrell.'

'I was just asking him if he had any paid work going,' Tim said, shifting uncomfortably, tightening his crossed arms.

'I won't tell the police what I saw.'

'What do you think you saw?'

'I don't know.'

'You tell the police what you need to tell them. Tell them you saw me at the fair if you want, or don't, it makes no odds to me. You don't have to lie for me,' Tim said, before disappearing into the pantry again.

Jasmine started to jot down the details of the night as she remembered them. Everything except seeing Tim at the fair before he came to rescue her by the beach. She had asked him not to tell her parents, and he hadn't, so she would keep his part in her story to a minimum. The police probably wouldn't care anyway so there was no need to drop him in it. He had respected her wishes and treated her as though she were old enough to make her own decisions and mistakes, and she didn't get a lot of that in this house. It was nice to finally have someone she could trust. It was nice to finally have an ally.

Chapter Nineteen

Overwhelmed by the events of the last few days, Jasmine had taken to her room to read a book. She needed a little escapism knowing what was coming since she had told her parents about bumping into Mr Morrell again. She had already spoken to the police but it wasn't over yet, not if last time was anything to go by. A gentle knock at the door disturbed her. She was annoyed before she even knew who it was or what they wanted. She just wanted to be alone.

'What is it?' she asked, sensing someone hovering on the other side of the bedroom door. She had no idea why someone would be up this early in the morning, let alone want to talk to her.

'It's Mum, would you come downstairs, please?'

'Have I got time to shower first?' she asked hopefully. The hair at the base of her scalp was wet, so were the wisps that usually tendrilled around her ears. Today they were sticking to her cheeks.

'If you must, but be quick,' her mother said, and Jasmine heard her walk away and down the stairs.

She had spent almost all day yesterday giving her statement to the police, as they questioned her over and over about who and what she'd seen at the fairground. They'd tried to poke holes in her story, as if she had any reason to lie to them. They'd also asked her lots of questions about Jason Evans, about what kind of person he was, and about Hannah Torrence – if she saw Mr Morrell talking to her at any point. The officers weren't familiar with Jasmine's case against Mr Morrell but when they discovered what had happened, their focus shifted and they became much more interested in him and why he was hanging around the fair. Maybe after Jasmine had rebuffed him he had gone after Hannah.

The police station had been completely airless and in the heat Jasmine had found it hard to concentrate. When they finally did get home, she had gone upstairs to bed and lain listening to music until she drifted off. This morning she wished she had taken the time to shower before she went to sleep; she felt positively grubby.

Jasmine grabbed a towel and jumped in the

shower, momentarily relieved. She twisted the tap, taking short, sharp breaths as the water got cooler, revelling in the feeling as it ran down her body, before she quickly washed her hair and got out again. Shivering, she dried herself, but the feeling only lasted a few seconds before the temperature of the room warmed her again. She pulled on a clean cotton night shirt and headed downstairs.

As she approached the kitchen, she heard her parents talking to someone. It became clear as she entered the room they were talking to a police officer, a different one to the ones she had spoken to yesterday.

'Jasmine. There you are,' Frank said, a look of deep concern on his face.

Jasmine flashed an angry look at her mother for not warning her, suddenly self-conscious about the nightshirt she was wearing, which had a cartoon panda on it. She tugged at the hem a little. At least the police officer was female.

'What's going on?' Jasmine asked. Surely they couldn't have any more questions about what had happened at the fair. Was she going to have to go into counselling again? The look on her parents' face told her it was about Mr Morrell. They had worn that look for most of last year.

'Hello, Jasmine, I need to speak to you about your former teacher, Mr Morrell.'

'What about him?' she said, glancing outside towards the guest house involuntarily. She felt like she was in a three against one situation.

'There's no easy way to say this.' The police officer, who hadn't even introduced herself, looked at her with a disturbing amount of concern. Jasmine wanted her to just say what she was there for. The suspense was unbearable. It was way too early for this.

'No easy way to say what?'

'Mr Morrell has taken his own life. Because of the restraining order and the notes on his file, I have been instructed to notify you.'

'What? When?'

Jasmine thought back to the fair. He'd seemed distressed when she'd seen him but it seemed completely out of character, not that Jasmine was sure she ever really knew what his character was. She felt as if he'd had more he needed to say to her.

'We found his body on the east side of the beach. It appears that after he was questioned yesterday he got drunk and jumped from the top.'

'He jumped? Is that high enough?'

'Apparently so.'

'Does she need to hear all of this?' her mother asked, trying to protect her from the wrong things as usual.

142

'It will be all over town soon enough. He was found by one of the parents from the school who was out fishing at the crack of dawn, so there's no keeping a lid on this. I just wanted to give you a heads-up,' the officer said.

'I'm supposed to be meeting my friends at the beach today. Everyone's going to be talking about me again. I haven't done anything wrong. I don't want to hide.' Jasmine could feel her chest tightening, the familiar anxiety she felt for most of last year creeping back. She was sorry about what had happened to Mr Morrell but this wasn't fair; she couldn't handle being the centre of everyone's conversations and dirty looks again.

'You don't have to go anywhere today,' Lisa said quickly.

'I'll be fine,' Jasmine lied. Today was going to be hell for her, but staying locked up inside was no alternative. Last time Jasmine had been vilified when he lost his job because of her, not just by students either. She knew a couple of teachers thought it was all her fault, that she had somehow encouraged him or led him on in some way.

'I know you gave a statement to the police already. But did Mr Morrell give any indication that he might do something like this?' the police officer asked.

She didn't know how to answer. His suicide

would now almost definitely be linked to Jasmine for ever. How was she supposed to know if he'd been suicidal?

'Are you saying she could have done something to help him? Maybe she should have just let him cop another feel and everything would have been fine. For fuck's sake. Do you not think maybe it was a bit insensitive to come here and suggest that my daughter's statement caused a man to commit suicide? Do you not think maybe it was his devious behaviour and twisted mind that was the problem?' Lisa snapped, reaching out for Jasmine's hand, which she pulled away. The police officer looked apologetic. This wasn't the kind of thing that happened much around here and so they probably didn't get much practice at being tactful.

'I need to get ready for the beach, if that's all? I told the police everything yesterday. I don't know anything else,' Jasmine said, walking away before anyone had a chance to stop her. She really didn't want to talk about it anymore. She tried to remember if Morrell had given any indication that he was thinking about ending his life, replaying that evening over and over in her mind. Then she remembered something else she hadn't told the police, something that seemed so inconsequential at the time, something that she had almost forgotten. She remembered the darkness in Tim's eyes when he'd glanced towards the cliff path; it had been chilling. When she got to her room she looked out of the window towards the guest house. Had Tim done this? Had he done it for her? Something about that idea excited her. She felt bad because she was glad Morrell was dead and she didn't want to say it out loud.

Chapter Twenty

The beach was, as Jasmine had suspected, a nightmare. The first few hours were fairly normal, but as the day went on and the news spread the looks and whispers got more obvious. The only thing that was stopping Jasmine from going home was the fact that her father had decided to work from home for the rest of the week just to make sure she was OK. She couldn't handle being around him all day.

'Want a drink?' Felicity asked, pulling a bottle of vodka out of her bag.

'Jesus, Flick, you'll drown if you go in the sea drunk.'

'Your loss,' Felicity said, knocking back the vodka as though it were water.

Felicity wore a red bikini and was getting just the amount of attention she wanted with it. A group of boys hovered nearby with music blasting also looking to get noticed. Felicity kept positioning herself in a way to get them to notice her and it was working. She stood up and walked over to the bin, throwing away something that didn't require the journey, but it gave her an opportunity to pass the boys and make sure they were fully aware of her.

She stood in front of Jasmine and scooped her jet black hair onto her head into a messy bun.

'Oh my God, Flick, you are shameless. I just want to chill and sit here for a bit.'

'Why do you care if he's dead? He's messed up things for you much more than you messed up things for him.'

'How do you figure that?'

'Well, he's out of it now, isn't he? You've still got to deal with this shit.'

'You really think he killed himself?'

'Don't you?' Felicity asked, tilting her head to one side, still with one eye on the boys. 'He just couldn't live without you,' she said in a fake sad voice.

Jasmine rolled her eyes and suppressed a smile. It didn't feel right to be smiling today. She couldn't talk about this with Felicity –

because Felicity's home life was genuinely quite unpleasant, she viewed most of Jasmine's problems as trivialities. Not to mention the fact that that vodka probably wasn't the first drink she had had today.

'Is this what you do all summer when I'm away?'

'There's nothing else to do bar sitting at home and trying and stop Mum's new boyfriend from coming on to me. If I'm going to get pawed I'd rather it was by someone my own age. You feel me? I know you do.'

'Flick!' Jasmine exclaimed, aware that Felicity was trying to lighten the mood the only way she knew how.

'It's too bloody hot. Are you coming in the sea?' Felicity shouted across to Jasmine, loud enough so the boys could hear.

'Are you sure that's a good idea?' Jasmine asked, nodding at the half-empty bottle of vodka lying on Felicity's towel.

'Help yourself if you want some. You need to relax a little!'

'I'm fine, thanks.'

'Well, come in when you're ready. You're going to look like a roast turkey if you stay out in this sun much longer.'

'Will do, if I don't go home,' Jasmine said, saluting at Felicity as she hobbled across the pebbles towards the sea. Three of the boys followed after her with their paddle boards, all a slightly alarming pink colour from being outside for too long. Felicity was right though, this was the only thing to do most of the time.

Jasmine wasn't sure she could take any more beach time. It was too hot for a start, but the looks she kept spying from the corner of her eye were really pissing her off. If it was just the kids her own age giving her daggers she might have been able to cope, but Mr Morrell's fiancée was there. She worked in a newsagent in town, and Jasmine knew what she looked like from when she had come to events at the school. They hadn't been engaged long when the incident happened last year. Now, his fiancée was on the beach looking wistfully out to sea and Jasmine could see she had been crying. Jasmine lay on a towel, the pebbles digging into her, occasionally looking over and seeing the woman's distraught and disapproving face.

Jasmine tried to suppress her nagging guilt about what Mr Morrell had done. She had told the police the truth about what happened with her former teacher at the fair; she had always told the truth about him. But by the end of the interrogation she'd felt as though she were the one who had committed the crime. The constant questions: Did he touch you? What did he say? Did you accidentally make him feel like that? She couldn't deal with that again. Jasmine knew that she hadn't made him take his own life, if that was even what had happened. Even if Tim had done something to him, she refused to feel like it was her fault in any way. She hadn't asked anyone to hurt him. She hadn't wanted any of this.

She glanced up at the cliffs. Even though he hadn't died here she could imagine him falling. How hard would it be to push someone off a cliff? And the pebbles below would put paid to any evidence on the skin. Not to mention Mr Morrell's recent history. Suicide would fit, wouldn't it? A nice, neat little box to put away and forget about, less scandalous than a murder.

Jasmine heard the crunch of the pebbles getting louder as someone walked towards her.

'Jasmine? Can I speak with you a moment?' Morrell's fiancée asked softly.

Jasmine heard the voices of the people around them simmer to a whisper, all waiting to see how she responded. She could tell they would all be watching her, waiting to see what might happen, hoping someone was going to get slapped in the face. Jasmine glanced at Felicity's vodka bottle and wished she had taken a drink after all.

'OK?' Jasmine said, sitting up.

'I hope you aren't being given too hard a time today.'

Jasmine was surprised by her kind tone; she had been expecting something else entirely. She wondered if she had any ability to read people at all.

'It's been a bit of a weird day,' Jasmine said, not knowing what else *to* say.

'If you need to talk then you can get in touch with me on my mobile. I know they really put you through the wringer last year because of what happened,' she said, handing Jasmine a scrap of paper with her name and a number scrawled on it.

'Thanks. I'm so sorry for your loss.'

'He was out of order last year, I know he was. I saw the video of what happened. I don't want you to think that what he did back then was OK and I also don't want you to blame yourself for him taking his own life. He's been depressed for a while.'

'Thanks,' Jasmine repeated, looking at the piece of paper with the woman's name on it. Elizabeth.

The tears appeared before she even had a chance to think about it. It meant something to hear those words from his fiancée, a woman who had no reason to be nice to her at all.

Maybe she was wrong; maybe people didn't blame her. Maybe she didn't understand people and she was actually projecting her own fears onto them. She was exhausted. She had spent the last hour and ten minutes paranoid that this woman hated her and it wasn't the case at all. Were other people good at this stuff? She decided to go home. She could call Felicity when she got there, as she didn't fancy drawing attention to herself by shouting out to the sea. It was too hot to stay out in the sun for any longer. Even though she was wearing factor fifty she could still feel her skin burning on her knees and shoulders. She grabbed her things and walked back up the slope, through the back gate onto the main road towards home.

She didn't want to be around anyone right now. But that wasn't entirely true. She felt like the only person on her side was Tim. He didn't tell her parents about what had happened at the fair even though it had got him into trouble. He had saved her from Mr Morrell. He was the only person she felt safe with, which was strange because she could tell he was dangerous. She couldn't understand why she wanted to see him when she thought he might have killed someone for her. Deep down inside him there was a big secret, and though she could see that it was there, she couldn't see what it was. She wanted to know though; she wanted to know him better. She could feel him pulling her towards home, towards him. No one else made sense right now.

Chapter Twenty-One

Now

I spend the afternoon into the evening talking to Jason. We walk along to the fort and stop in a café, where we drink multiple coffees on the terrace. He tells me he has never been married but he briefly dated a girl who had been in the year below us in school. She cheated on him and is now married with three children. He talks about it as though he has dodged a bullet, but I can see that he is lonely. He seems reluctant to let me go and, if I am honest, I'm reluctant to leave him alone. I guess he wishes his life had gone differently too. In a way, when Hannah went missing it was the beginning of the end for a lot of us. It certainly shook the town and the way everyone perceived our little sanctuary. Suddenly curfews were imposed, whereas before we could walk home in the dark with no one batting an eye, our parents confident that this sleepy little oasis held no hidden monsters. Whether they were in denial or whether they were just naive, I don't think I will ever really know. Possibly a mixture of both. All I know is that nothing could have prepared me for what happened. That's why when the summer was over I ran and never stopped.

Jason was one of the ones left behind, and even though he now has no ties, he doesn't speak like a person with any designs on leaving the place. Even given the way he was treated in the couple of days after Hannah disappeared, until the police discovered her wallet and clothing fibres in Mr Morrell's car. Jason tells me that one of the other teachers at our school has gone to prison for having indecent images of children on his computer. Mr Goss. I remember him, so friendly, always trying to be everyone's friend. You really never know what's going on inside people. Even when you think you know them they turn out to be someone else. Some*thing* else. I want more for Jason than this. I feel responsible somehow. As if I have the answers. As if my secrets are the reason he is still here.

'What do you think happened to Hannah?' I ask, seeing no point in not being direct.

'I don't know. I've thought about it a million times. I don't believe she would have got into a car with that guy, she wasn't stupid.'

'You don't think he killed her?'

'I mean, maybe . . . I don't know, I really don't. I don't even think she knew who he was. That's like self-preservation 101, isn't it? Don't get into a car with a bloke you don't know?'

'Or a woman,' I add. I don't know why.

'I know some people still think it was me that did it.'

'Why do you stay here?'

'I don't have any qualifications. I failed my exams. This is the best it gets for me.'

'Do you own your house?'

'Totally and utterly. My parents paid the mortgage off a few years before they died and business has been better in the last couple of years, since cycling became a super trendy thing to do.'

'So sell it all and go. Just start again where no one knows you. That's what I would do. That's what I *did* do.'

'And you're happy?'

'Now there's a question. I know one thing though. Getting away from here was the best thing I ever did,' I say, and although I don't regret leaving for a second, I realise I never really got away. A part of me will always remain here; coming back made me see I could never escape completely. I hope things will be different for Jason though; he doesn't have the same demons that I have.

'Where would I go? What would I do?'

'Well, I don't know the answer to that, but cycling is something that people do all over the world. I remember seeing a documentary about a town in Wisconsin that is one of the most bike-friendly places on earth. My husband is into biking, too, so we watch things like that. I think it was called Madison. I bet you could go there.'

'I don't know about that.'

'What is keeping you here, Jason? What exactly are you doing here? Sell your stuff and get out. A handsome young English man in America – I bet you would do great over there. Just think about it,' I say, knowing that he has no intention of doing so. This place has its hooks in him; he will never get away. At least I tried, at least I planted the seed.

I pull out my phone and look for a real estate agent in Madison.

'You really think that's possible?'

'Look at this. I don't know the city at all but this house is two hundred thousand; I bet your place is worth much more than that – there isn't much around here that isn't. Sell the business too and you'll have enough to plonk yourself there instead of here and you have a brand new life ready to go. The great lakes are there too. It would be amazing.'

I show him my phone, displaying a colonial-looking, grey, two-bedroom house with one of those porch verandas with a swing seat that always make me so jealous.

He laughs and a big smile breaks out across his face. He actually needed someone to point out to him that he deserved more than this existence of getting high on his own in the back of an empty bike shop.

'Are you really here?'

'What do you mean?'

'Today has been weird, almost like a dream. A few hours with you and I feel completely different. If only we had been friends all those years ago. Maybe things could have been different. No one has had this profound an effect on me in such a short space of time.'

'I promise I'm real.'

'Well, thank you, Felicity "Icantrememberyourlastname", I think you might be my guardian angel or something. A beacon of light in the monotony of my daily existence.'

'I just think you could do so much more. Don't settle for what life gives you.'

He leans over and kisses me on the mouth, tender but not sleazy in any way, like a full stop at the end of a sentence. I don't know why but I don't recoil. He pulls away and looks down, embarrassed.

'Sorry, I just wanted to check you were really here. Cheeky, I know.'

'Well, it was nice seeing you again, Jason. I have to get back to my hotel now.'

'I have to go play Warcraft with my guild,' he says with a grin. 'You know, you've changed a lot. You're not like the girls who stayed here, you seem more alive somehow.'

If only he knew how wrong he was.

My first interaction with someone from the past has been a positive one and I really wasn't expecting it to go that way. In my mind I had built this place up as my own personal axis of evil, where everything and everyone was out to get me.

I am tired and I am hungry. I watch as Jason disappears around the corner and head back towards town to get another drink.

In the pub I get a sandwich for dinner; it's a fancy one served on a wooden board with a smattering of leaves on the side. I look at my phone;

no calls from Chris today. That voice in the back of my head tells me he's just keeping me around out of sympathy, even though I know that's stupid. I don't want to indulge in my self-doubt right now, so I go back to the bar and order a drink, just a half of beer this time. When I get there the bar staff, a young man with a name badge that says Paul and a woman my age called Flora, are chatting in hushed tones.

'Do they know who it is?' Flora asks.

'It's got to be her, hasn't it?' Paul replies.

'How sure are you about it?'

'I told you my brother works in the pub there and there's police everywhere. They found a body.'

The words ring out in my ears. Am I too late? I had hoped that maybe I could have found out something first; like maybe I could have saved her if I just figured out what was going on.

'Excuse me,' I interrupt, 'did you say they found a body? Do you mean the Green girl?'

'Yes, they had the cadaver dogs up at the Bulverton Woods and they found something,' Paul responds.

'Is it her?' I ask.

'Who else is it going to be?' Paul says.

It could be anyone. I don't think anyone realises the secrets buried in this little valley town.

I pay for my food and leave. I remember what

a nightmare it is to get taxis around here so I rush back to the hotel to pick up the car. I know I shouldn't drive, I know I am over the limit, but I need to know what they found in the woods. I don't know how close I can even get, but I have to try.

I jog most of the way to the hotel, which isn't the greatest idea after a day of vodka and beer. My head feels fuzzy. I take the keys and get in the car. At least there is a bottle of water in the space between the seats. It's half finished and I don't know how long it's been in the car, but I don't really care about the bacteria at this point. I drink the water in the hope that it will sober me up a little. I don't feel drunk, but I know how much I have had over the course of the day. I didn't think I would need to drive.

I pull out of the hotel car park and into the road, past the terrace where I was sitting with Jason and up the road towards the Bulverton Woods. I don't know why I feel so urgent about getting there when she is already dead, but I need to know for sure that she is gone, that there is no hope for her. Maybe one of the police officers will speak to me. The traffic on the way to the woods is tight and slows at the bottleneck with All Saints Road. I can feel myself getting closer to both the woods and the street my old family

162

home is on. I wanted to avoid seeing it if I could. I know I shouldn't, but I close my eyes as I drive past the turning, tears falling. I can't help but wonder what it looks like now; I wonder if the years of neglect have been unkind. A part of me hopes the place has been swallowed into the ground.

I see the lights before I reach the woods. An intermittent flashing blue that varies in intensity, so out of place here in the dark. I pull over as I get closer, realising that I am approaching a sea of police cars and I am very much over the limit. I grab a mint from the glove box and pull my hair in front of my face, afraid of being recognised yet again, afraid of who else I might bump into.

I can't even get close but I stand as near as I can, wishing I had a dog or something to excuse myself as a passer-by. No one used to just go for a walk up here without a purpose of some kind, not in this area where you had the beautiful coast-line nearby, and most definitely not this time of night. My very presence here puts me in danger; if the police start asking questions I don't know if I have the energy to lie any more. So many people got away with so many things that summer, I would hate to think it was happening again. Hannah's disappearance was the end for her; would this discovery in the woods signify the end for some other poor girl? They never found Hannah's body. I always wondered where it was, because the only thing I ever knew for certain was that she was dead. I could tell them the things I do know but, on reflection, it isn't much, nothing I can tell the police without sounding crazy. I could tell them that I keep seeing ghosts. But if I put myself forward then my life as I know it is over. Chris would never forgive me and my children would see me as a monster. So I stay camouflaged and pressed against a hedgerow. I see the officers busying themselves and the feeling of their excitement is real. They have a result. They have found a body. I can feel the wind turning, as though a big change is coming. For so long things have been off kilter, things have been out of place. The puzzle pieces that have been scattered for so long are starting to slot back into their rightful places. I can't see the full picture yet but I know I will before long. The discovery of a body changes the rules of this game somewhat. People will pay attention now. Things like that just don't happen around here. Do they?

Chapter Twenty-Two

Everything happens so quickly on television it's easy to forget that in real time there are no editors there to cut out all the surplus and leave it on the cutting room floor. I wait for a good hour before a team turns up to dig the body out of the ground. I heard the officers talking; they needed a specialist to do the excavation to preserve evidence. There is no one even remotely equipped to deal with a job like this nearby and at this time of night. It will probably be a few more hours before a formal identification is made and I wonder if there is any way I can get closer without being seen. What am I even doing here? I should get on a plane and get as far away as humanly possible. I have a passport with me. Would anyone even miss me at this point? The fact that Chris still hasn't called just proves how well everyone does without me. I don't know who or what they might find in these woods. I don't know if it will link back to me in any way. The thought of being questioned by the police makes me feel nauseous.

I sneak closer to see if they know anything, to see if I need to run again. I can't hear any conversations; maybe it's time to call it a night. I start to walk back to my car, an uneasy feeling following me – but that's nothing new.

As I get closer to my car I can hear the rumble of a vehicle but I can't see it. Is it even possible that I recognise the sound of the engine? I start to walk faster, sure that there is someone there. There is no parallel road here so the car must be behind me. I can see no headlights. I feel the panic rising and instead of walking faster I duck behind a tree and wait as the sound gets louder, closer. There on the road is an old brown car, just like the one they said went past on the night Mandy Green went missing. It's shrouded in darkness so I can't quite see who is driving. I know this car though, or I think I do. I have been drinking; can I even trust my eyes? The car rolls past and I wait behind the tree until I can hear nothing again. The blue lights still thump against the sky in the near distance, but the road is empty again. I get back in my car and pull a U-turn. I can't investigate anything like this. I need to sleep it off.

I get back to the hotel smack in the middle of the night. I wonder what the concierge thinks I might have been doing all this time. I don't know why this place brings out the worst in me. I don't know why I can't go an hour without a drink when I am here. Once in my room, I throw my clothes onto the floor and look out of the window. There's no one there, but I imagine someone is watching me. I climb into the bed and wait for sleep, a million questions swimming around in my head. I should just get back in the car when I wake up and go back home. This was all a big mistake and I feel like I am on the brink of destroying myself by being here. I am putting everything and everyone I love in danger because I couldn't stay away. I was gone, I was free. But the pull was too much. Curiosity killed the cat. I just hope it doesn't kill me.

Chapter Twenty-Three

I have missed the morning again. I wake up and my head is pounding, My minibar is empty apart from a Kit-Kat, which I eat greedily, hoping the sugar does something to alleviate the pain in my temples, which of course it doesn't. I instinctively pick up my phone to check if Chris has called me. He hasn't. I feel more alone than ever in this stupid hotel room. I dismiss my viewing of the brown car as nothing but my mind playing tricks on me. It wouldn't be the first time. God knows I haven't been myself for a long time. The car is just another ghost, the man who drove that car barely a memory anymore; why would he be following me? Why here and why now? Our paths crossed so briefly in the grand scheme of things but he was the catalyst. He was the beginning of the end.

I jump in the shower and wash away the sins of yesterday, determined to be a better me today, determined to stay sober at the very least. It's past lunch by the time I leave the hotel wearing trainers and leggings, with my cardigan pulled tight around me. As I walk along the promenade I break out into a run, needing that feeling of freedom just for a moment, the feeling of moving too fast for anyone to catch up to me. The wind at my heels and the sea on my right. As I near the town I slow again, shifting my gaze to the ground in order to avoid eye contact, resuming my position as a stranger.

I pick a small café in town and order myself an espresso. There is a local newspaper on the next table; well-worn with the crosswords already filled in. I grab it and scan it for information about the body they found but there's no mention of it. When the waitress brings me my coffee I try to act as normal as I can manage.

'Is there any news about what they found up in the woods? Was it that girl?'

'I'm sorry. They haven't said anything yet. Might be on the telly news this afternoon. Things move slowly round here. Paper only comes out once a week.'

'Thank you.'

I think about going up to the Spar where Mandy Green's mother works again, but it feels a bit intrusive. I lived all this before, but where I was just visiting ghosts this was really happening for her and I needed to keep that in mind. It wasn't all about me. And besides, I might be completely mistaken about what I think is happening, inserting my own bias into everything. I have to find out what's going on. Like the lady said, everything moves at a snail's pace around here.

I pull out my phone and look up a picture of Mandy Green online. *Have you seen this girl?* She looks a bit like Hannah. Is that why she was taken? Is that the connection? Long brown hair and definitely from a certain demographic, a little goth-y, a little angry looking, the kind of girl whose absence might take a little longer to notice and report.

The girl who served me my coffee comes back over to the table. I expect her to ask me if everything is all right with my order, because that's what they always ask, but she doesn't. She slides into the chair opposite me and leans forward, making sure no one else can hear, possibly not wishing to risk disturbing the other customers.

'It wasn't her in the woods. It wasn't Mandy.'

'How do you know?' I say, relieved for the most part but also confused. Who could it be?

'It was just on the radio. They said it was a false alarm.'

'Do you know her?' I ask, realising they must be a similar age.

'A bit. Not really,' she says. I feel relieved.

'So, it was a false alarm. They didn't find a body?'

'Oh, they found a body, it just wasn't Mandy's.'

'It wasn't? Did they say who they think it is?' I ask, not sure if I am ready to hear whatever she is about to say.

'No, but apparently it had been there for years.'

I pull back, her words completely unexpected – even though it was something I had feared. I had assumed that Hannah's fate would always remain a mystery, and the thought that she may have been found felt strange. I always suspected whatever had happened to Hannah, she couldn't have been buried far away. Was it her body in the woods? What if it wasn't? Maybe there were more skeletons in this town than anyone was prepared for.

Chapter Twenty-Four

Then

It was still unbearably warm outside and Jasmine had sweated through the shorts and T-shirt that she had worn to the beach so she picked out her indigo tie-dyed summer dress, with thin straps and a nipped-in waist. Lisa had bought it a few years ago in Honduras. A safety pin held the strap in place at the back, but Jasmine still loved it. She put her slouch boots on and looked in the mirror, tousling her hair so it looked full and framed her face. The sun had lightened the front slightly and so her golden brown hair was even more golden than usual. Her parents were still at work and she glanced into the back garden, which was empty apart from the neighbour's cat Malcolm, perched on the roof of the guest house. She could see that the wall was finished now, and her mother's geraniums were on a tiered wooden shelving unit. She was a little scared to go outside in case Tim came out, although maybe it wasn't fear that she was feeling but excitement, anticipation. She pushed those feelings aside for now; they were friends, that's all. She grabbed a new book from the shelf and braved her way downstairs and out into the garden.

She lay on the sun lounger under the white calico parasol, her legs exposed to the sunshine, the skirt of her dress hitched up a little to make sure she tanned evenly. She kicked her boots onto the ground and opened the book. She had dark shades on so that her eyes were free to roam, to look over to the door of the guest house if it opened, while still maintaining the appearance of someone who didn't care. She felt like a spy on a covert operation, a secret mission to gather as much information as she could on their mysterious lodger. On her way downstairs she'd seen his tatty brown car parked outside the front of the house, so she knew he was in the guest house. She wondered if he was awake, or if he was having an afternoon nap. He didn't work regular hours; he just helped people as and when. He usually got up so early that she wouldn't be surprised if he had to rest in the middle of the day. She found herself wondering how he slept, what he wore. She caught her breath at the thought of him lying in his bed, before quickly pushing that image aside. As she started to drift off to sleep, imagining him stretched out on his mattress, her book thumped against her chest, waking her.

She heard the toilet flush inside the guest house, and she was instantly alert. He was walking around now. She imagined him with his jeans hanging on his hips, unbuttoned, his hair a mess. Whenever she saw him, he was always so well presented with his hair combed back and away from his face, but she knew when he was alone that probably wasn't the case and she thought she might like to see him a little messy. She wondered what his hair would feel like to the touch, his skin. She wondered if he ever thought those things about her. Since he had rescued her from Mr Morrell she'd found herself thinking of him as her knight in shining armour, and it was increasingly hard not to get carried away with it. He probably thought of her as some kid, if he even thought of her at all. She had seen him look at her mother before, when he thought no one was looking. Did he think about Lisa in the way Jasmine thought about him? She couldn't stand the thought of it. She wished she was older; she wished she wasn't invisible to him.

Her breathing, which had been shallow for a while now, got faster as she heard the seal on the door to the guest house release as he pushed the handle down. She pretended to look at her book but really she was watching him. He didn't look at her once. He was wearing the jeans she imagined he would be wearing, and a crisp, fitted, white T-shirt, the short sleeves folded over a couple of times, exposing the tops of his arms. He went straight to the shed and pulled out the lawn-mower. She watched him pulling on the cord to start it, the muscles in his slender arms tightening as he gripped the metal pull at the end of the wire. She forgot to turn the pages of her book. The sun burned her thighs, but she didn't want to move lest she alerted him to her presence. He leaned against the handle of the mower as he walked, and his shoulders bulged a little at the back. It was so warm and already the centre of his shirt was slightly darker where he was sweating. He continued to mow the lawn and she continue to ignore her book.

'What you reading?' he called out to her over the sound of the lawnmower. She was startled by the sudden interaction.

She had to check the cover as she couldn't even

remember; she hadn't looked at the pages for quite some time.

'*Slaughterhouse Five.*'

'Is that homework?'

He thought of her as a child, as though she couldn't be reading a book like this of her own volition. As though she would have to be forced to read such a text. She felt a little angry that he couldn't see past her age.

'No, I just heard it was good.'

He smiled but there was something false about it, she didn't believe it. There was something sad about him, something broken. She couldn't put her finger on it until she realised – his eyes stayed flat even though his grin spread wide.

He stopped the lawn-mower and sat on the lounger next to her. Her body tensed at the proximity. He leaned forward, placing his elbows on his knees. His face was shaded but he still had that squint as he looked at her. She pulled her sunglasses off.

'Are you OK today? After the other night?'

'Did you hear what happened?'

'Hear what?'

She lowered her voice and leaned forward. 'The man from that night, my teacher, he committed suicide. He jumped off the cliff. I went to the beach with my friend earlier but everyone is talking about it and so I decided to come home and hang out here. The police came and spoke to me about it this morning,' she said, trying to see if he reacted at all to the news. His face remained unchanged. Maybe she was wrong about what she had seen.

'And you spoke to the police?'

'I told them everything I could remember. Did they speak to you yet?'

'Are you upset that he's dead?' he said quietly. She could see a flicker of something behind his eyes as he stared at her. It was the thing that was missing when he smiled. A little wickedness maybe.

Could she trust him and tell him the truth? There was something about him that commanded it. Even though she could feel his dishonesty with every movement of his lips, she still couldn't lie to him.

'No, I don't think I am,' she said quietly. She felt excited as she said it, as if she was telling him a big secret. Another secret that they shared.

'I told you that you would be safer now.' He smiled. She couldn't help thinking of it as a confession of some kind, a nod to some action he had taken, just for her.

'So you're off to college next year?' he asked, changing the subject, breaking the invisible string that she felt pulling her towards him sometimes.

'After the summer is over, just in the city,' she said, wishing he wouldn't keep mentioning the fact that she was at school.

'And you spend your summers on the beach or in the garden?'

'We usually go abroad to do charity projects in underprivileged countries, but we can't this year because of my dad's surgery.'

She felt stupid as she said it; it was her parents' thing and she just tagged along.

'That's very noble of you and your parents.' He smiled that dead smile again, something else behind his eyes. Something dark that made her regret her momentary loss of composure.

'They do most of the work.'

His face lightened again and it was as if that last slip of his mask had never happened.

'You shouldn't be so hard on yourself. Anyone with eyes can see that you're not like other girls. I bet you've got really big plans for your future.'

She didn't know how to respond to that comment. He was still squinting and looking straight at her. Was this another case of her not understanding the subtext of what someone was trying to say?

'I don't really know what I want to do.'

'Must be nice to have a future. Mummy and Daddy looking out for you, making sure nothing bad happens. Well, Daddy wasn't there the other night, was he? I was the one who kept you safe. I was the one who made sure that man didn't hurt you.'

After a few moments of staring, the corner of his mouth broke into a side smile. He smacked his hands on his knees and went back to the lawn-mower. He looked at her as he started the engine again.

She sat forward and pulled her boots back on before getting up and walking into the kitchen to fix herself a drink. His words circled in her mind. Was he confessing to her that he had hurt Mr Morrell? Did he do that for her? She tried to ignore the feeling of excitement that bubbled under her skin. It wasn't the only thing she could feel but she chose to ignore that even more.

Chapter Twenty-Five

Jasmine watched the guest house from the bedroom window as she lay on her bed. She kept her lights out and propped her head up on her pillows, her eyelids growing heavy as she concentrated on the dim light until it went out. Apart from those first few conversations when she thought Tim was flirting with her, his intentions seemed to have changed completely now. She wasn't even sure if the conversation she had had with him in the garden about Mr Morrell had actually happened. Maybe it was all in her mind.

Her parents were going away this weekend and were trusting her to stay home alone for the most part. Except she wouldn't be alone as Felicity was staying over. No doubt Felicity would turn on the charm and her visit would be completely dominated by trying to get Tim's attention. What's more, she would succeed. Jasmine had seen it a hundred times before. Felicity liked to stay at Jasmine's house and play happy families whenever she could. Jasmine rarely went to stay at hers. Carol, Felicity's mother, was not really a mother at all, more like a sibling who had been forced into babysitting and rebelled against that at every opportunity. At her house there were always drug paraphernalia on the table and no shortage of drinks. You wouldn't know any of this to look at Felicity – she did a remarkable job of acting confident – but sometimes she was a little over-eager, a little too overbearing with it, trying too hard to be like everyone else.

After what had happened at the fair Jasmine's parents had obviously decided that Tim was trustworthy enough to be left alone with her for two nights. Since Jasmine had turned fourteen, they had these little weekends away every few months. They had always said she needed the opportunity to show them she could be trusted. Usually she just set up a projector in their old back yard and she and Felicity would watch horror movies together. It wasn't herself she was worried about this time though, it was Tim. Every time she decided he was on the level, he did or said something to make her think otherwise. Were her parents completely oblivious to his strange behaviour?

She heard her parents leave for work before she stepped outside of her room. She didn't want to speak to them. All they wanted to talk about these last couple of days were her feelings and whether she was sure she didn't need to see a counsellor about what happened to Mr Morrell. She could tell they were glad he was dead, too. She wasn't mad at them for being concerned but she found it strange that they hadn't picked up on how odd Tim was. Half scared and half excited by Tim's presence, she had started to make up little scenarios in her head of Tim finding ways to spend time with her, finding ways to be in the room with her.

When she came downstairs the kitchen was empty, but her mother had left a toasted sandwich on the counter for her. There was a note on the fridge, a list of instructions for the weekend. She would read it later. She picked up the sandwich and went to stand by the French doors to the garden. She watched the guest house from the corner of her eye while she ate. To her surprise the door opened and Tim came outside. She wasn't ready for this. He walked over to the house and stared straight at her. He had a very leisurely stride, swinging his arms and tilting his head to the side as he moved, always squinting a little. He knocked on the door and Jasmine opened it.

'Your dad asked me to check if you had rehearsals tonight or something and need me to take you after school?'

'No. They haven't started yet; I told him that already. I'll be home at the usual time. My friend Felicity is coming to stay tonight.'

'Great.' He pushed the door to close it.

'Do you want some breakfast?' Jasmine blurted without thinking. She wanted to ask him about the night at the fair and this was the first opportunity she had had. 'I could make you a cheese toastie.'

'Thanks, that would be nice.'

She walked over to the cupboard and pulled the toasted sandwich maker out. It was still a little warm from when her mother had used it earlier. Tim walked over to the counter and leaned against it, folding his arms. His biceps bulged a little and she tried not to look. He was fit but not muscular. His slender body was at least a foot taller than her own and she wondered if that was why he seemed to lean back in any scenario, to seem smaller and less intimidating. His eyes were always slightly narrowed, almost squinting, like he was scrutinising everything; it was another thing about him that made her suspicious.

She buttered the bread, all the while aware of him watching her.

'Did you go back out after you brought me home the night of the fair?' she asked, trying to sound nonchalant.

'No. I went to bed. Why would I go back out?'

'I don't know, I just wondered if you saw Mr Morrell again after you found me with him.'

She looked at him, trying to see if he was giving anything away but he never did and now was no exception.

'I saw you at the fair talking to someone, then you disappeared again. Then what happened with Mr Morrell happened. It was really lucky you turning up when you did.'

'Do you think I'm following you? Why would I do that?' He stood up straighter, making her feel smaller, more vulnerable. She looked at him again and he was looking straight at her, which made her think maybe she was being paranoid about the whole thing. Mr Morrell's appearance out of nowhere was more suspicious than Tim's; the teacher was probably lying in wait for a chance to talk to her. Maybe her constant suspicion of Tim was unfair and just a by-product of her encounters with Morrell.

'Do you want tomato in it?'

'No. I like the roof of my mouth as it is, thanks,'

he said, his voice softening, shifting the tone of the conversation.

She laughed a little and he smiled, and all she could do was concentrate on breathing because she wanted to hold her breath. The sandwich was in the toaster and they were both waiting for the cheese to drip out of the sides, which was how she knew it was done. Jasmine looked at the clock. She was going to miss her bus, but she didn't care if she was late. The silence was awkward; she could feel him trying to look anywhere but at her. She wondered why that was. The dynamic between them was strange, as though they were both slightly wary of one another. He was trying to read her as much as she was trying to read him. Although she knew it didn't make sense and although she knew there was something dangerous about him, it didn't feel directed at her. He deserved the benefit of the doubt, didn't he?

She put the sandwich on the plate and looked at the clock again. She had less than five minutes to get her bag, get her shoes on and get to the bus stop. She was dreading putting on the school blazer, which didn't seem to be made for either hot or cold weather.

'You keep looking at that clock. Am I making you late?' Tim asked as she handed him the sandwich.

'I'll get the next bus,' she replied as their eyes connected for a brief moment. His eyes were a dark blue today, like a thunder cloud. They seemed to be different every time she caught them.

'I can drive you.'

The thought of sitting next to him in the car excited her, like she was doing something she shouldn't. She felt like she was at the beginning of one of her daydreams as this was how they started, a situation that she hadn't engineered where they got to be alone together in a confined space.

'Thank you.'

'Let's go.'

She followed behind and watched him. He checked up and down the street before getting in his car. She wondered what he was looking for. As he changed gears, she noticed he was wearing a handwoven friendship bracelet. Jasmine thought that was the kind of gift you would be given by a girl, so her mind went into overdrive. Did he have a girlfriend? She had never even seen him speaking on the phone, but who knew what he did when he was alone in his room. Or the bracelet could be from a sister. Before she could ask about it, they were at the school. Felicity was standing at the gate and her eyes widened as she saw Jasmine get out of Tim's car. Tim got out too, and leaned against the door jamb.

'Who's your friend?' Tim asked, his crocodile smile in full effect.

'I'm Flick,' Felicity said. 'Are you Jazz's lodger?'

'Something like that.'

Jasmine couldn't help but feel tense at this interaction; Felicity always did know how to wrap males around her finger and Tim was someone Jasmine wanted to keep just for herself. Something sank inside her as they looked at each other; there was an instant ember there. At home, she hadn't really been able to tell what she felt about Tim – she was torn between being grateful that he had intervened with Mr Morrell and being suspicious of his stranger behaviours. Seeing the way he was sparking with Felicity invoked a new feeling entirely. She was jealous.

'I'll see you later,' Jasmine said to Tim, obviously hoping he would take his leave. He did a little salute as though he understood her instruction. She looked away quickly and he got back in the car and started the engine. Felicity pretend-screamed in excitement as Jasmine approached her, and she hoped that Tim couldn't hear. She was so embarrassed, but when she turned back to look, his car was gone. He didn't watch Jasmine to the last possible second like she watched him.

Chapter Twenty-Six

Now

I sit in front of the beach huts by Jacob's Ladder. I have my big shades on. The beach doesn't seem as clean as I remember it, but there is no arguing that the view is stunning. There is something about the sea, it's magnetic. I had forgotten, in my haste to get away from it, what it felt like to be near it. Our house is near Brothers Water lake, named after two boys who drowned there. Although it's a morbid name it's a pretty place, especially in the spring when the flowers on the banks are in bloom. The sea is a different beast though, less quiet, less contained, less predictable. It's warm today so it's calm, but I have seen it at its angriest and most spiteful. Underestimate it at your peril.

Watching people with their children makes me think of my own. Chris still hasn't called me. I think he's making a point. I wish he would tell me what it is. I check the local news on my phone, but there's still no identification of the body they found in the woods, just regurgitations of other accounts that I have already seen. They have been digging up there all through the night. I look for any mention of a brown car being spotted, hoping to find something to corroborate what I think I have seen. There are mentions of a car in the press but one cites it as maroon and another beige, both adding to my confusion. I am surprised the discovery of the body hasn't made the national news, but the usual political shenanigans are overshadowing every other thing on the planet. As the media whip themselves into a frenzy about who said what to whom, Mandy Green's murder goes unmentioned since that first report. If I hadn't been watching the news at that exact moment I wouldn't have known about this and I wouldn't have come here. A part of me wishes I had never seen it at all.

I haven't touched any alcohol today. I was stupid yesterday, self-indulgent, afraid of the past. Meeting with Jason proved I didn't need to be afraid, that people remember only what applies to them, which I am guilty of myself. I lied when I told Jason I didn't remember the party where everyone played spin the bottle. I didn't want him to think too much about me and who I used to be. The me he remembers had a terrible reputation at school. It took a long time to reinvent myself after leaving.

Knowing what it's like in the summer, I came to the beach at Jacob's Ladder. It's where most people go to swim as there is sand when the sea pulls back away from the pebbles while the tide is out. I scan the beach for familiar faces, no longer afraid of being discovered. Although Jason was high when I spoke to him, I think the meeting went well and proved that maybe I have been afraid unduly. I notice some women around my age gathered with a group of children and toddlers and watch them intently, getting closer so that I can hear their names. The one in the middle is called Claire; I remember her. We were never friends but she may remember me enough to talk to me.

I take off my shoes and get up to walk towards the sea, past the women and through a toddler's sandcastle.

'Oh gosh, I'm so sorry,' I say as I kick through one of the towers.

The child immediately bursts into tears at the sight of the destroyed moat and towers.

'It doesn't matter, it's nothing, really.' The woman, Claire, jumps up and rushes over to him, quickly scooping him up and smiling at me.

'I didn't even notice it,' I lie.

'This is going to sound really weird, but do I know you? You seem really familiar,' Claire says, checking me up and down.

'I don't know, I'm not local.' I swallow hard and hope she doesn't just dismiss me. I feel like she is more likely to open up to me if she doesn't think I'm interrogating her.

'No, there's definitely something familiar about you. My name is Claire Thorpe, I used to be Claire Woods. Did you go to school with me?'

'Oh, maybe. I used to live here. My name's Felicity . . .'

'Felicity! Flick! I knew I remembered you. They used to call you Fuck, because when you wrote your name out in cursive that's what it looked like.' Claire blushes as she speaks. 'Why do I remember that? God, I'm sorry.'

'It's fine.' I laugh; I had actually forgotten about that.

'Why don't you come sit with us?' she asks, gesturing to another woman with a small child, who waves back at us when she sees Claire pointing. I smile at the other woman.

'OK.'

I sit with these two women I barely knew at school, hoping they are more interested in talking about themselves than asking me questions. Claire has straightened blonde hair to her shoulders and a full face of make-up; she obviously has no intention of getting in the sea. The other woman has a similar haircut; they probably have the same hairdresser. I feel a little jealous as I miss having a best friend; it's been a long time – unless you count Chris, which I do but it really isn't the same. They both have small children and I think about my own, and how young I was when I had Daisy. I wish I had brought Daisy and Lloyd with me. I feel sad that I have to keep this part of myself from them.

'Do you remember Flick?' Claire says to her friend, who I don't recognise at all. 'Flick, this is Jenny Rawlings.'

'A bit, I guess. We didn't really talk much,' Jenny says, one eye on her toddler, who is trying to steal another child's pebble collection, despite the millions of pebbles in the immediate vicinity.

'Are you down for the summer?' Claire asks.

'No, just a week.'

'Well, you picked a hell of a week. It's been all drama all the time,' Claire says excitedly.

'I noticed, it's crazy.'

'Our Neil said they have had loads of overtime

and they have even brought in some outside police to deal with all the stuff they have going on,' Jenny tells me, clearly desperate to do some gossiping.

'Where did you move to then?' Claire asks.

'I moved to The Lake District. Got married, had two kids, the whole shebang.'

'Wow. I went to a wedding up at Lake Windermere a few years ago and it was absolutely stunning. You lucky thing,' Claire says. She is a lot friendlier than I remember her being at school. But in school you stick to your cliques and just assume no one knows what you are going through. Of course, in my case, it was true.

'Your husband's in the police?' I say to Jenny, finally processing what she said before.

'Well, partner, we aren't married. Yeah, he's a police officer.'

'Is he working on the missing girl case?'

'Everyone is. They thought they found her up at the Bully Woods, but it was someone else.'

'I heard on the radio. No identification?' I say. I can see that Jenny is excited at being questioned, like she is the holder of something precious and rare, like she is some kind of dealer. She leans in, a twinkle in her eye. Whispering as though she has never told anyone this before, which we all know isn't true.

'I shouldn't say but seeing as you aren't from

round here anyway, I guess there's no harm. It was someone who had been there a few years so it couldn't be her.'

I hope this isn't the limit of her information as I already knew that bit of gossip. Thankfully, I can see that she has more.

'Do they know who it is?'

'Not exactly, but they did find some dog tags. Neil didn't get a look at them so that's all I know,' Jenny says excitedly.

I feel a little sick as I hear about the dog tags. That could be a coincidence, surely.

'There's no way it's Mandy Green, that's all I know. Maybe there's a whole load of bodies up there in those woods,' Claire says.

'Don't be so morbid!' Jenny laughs.

'Was it a girl's body?' I don't want to press her any more about the dog tags directly; I think it would look weird. I'm almost certain Jenny is telling us absolutely everything she knows just to keep our focus on her. I get the impression she is very rarely the centre of attention.

'Probably. Who knows? The killer must have dropped the tags in there,' Jenny says dismissively, waving her hand. She watches as her child destroys another child's sandcastle.

'Do you keep in touch with anyone else from school?' Claire asks me.

'No, not at all.'

'What about that girl you were always hanging around with – the little hippy chick?' Jenny says.

'That was Jasmine Burgess. Oh, I remember her. She was the one who had that affair with the English teacher. What was his name?' Claire says.

'Nah, he assaulted her, didn't he? #MeToo and all that. Do you ever see her?' Jenny asks.

'I haven't spoken to anyone from school since I moved away. Apart from Jason Evans, I spoke to him yesterday.'

'Oh, he was an oddball for sure. I wouldn't be surprised if he was the one who took that Mandy Green girl,' Jenny says confidently.

'Have the police even questioned him?' Claire asks.

'Didn't need to. One of the guys in Neil's squad was in a pool tournament with him on the night she went missing. He probably would have been suspect number one otherwise,' Jenny confides.

'So he had a proper alibi and you still think it was him? That hardly seems fair,' I say, trying not to sound too judgmental.

'Well, they thought that teacher took Hannah Torrence, but they never found a body and he didn't confess before committing suicide. I was just never convinced. That teacher got a bit of a raw deal if you ask me. I reckon it's possible Jason did it. Kind of suspicious how Jason was the last person to see Hannah alive. I never liked him, to be honest.' Jenny says and Claire nods sagely, as if they have figured something out that no one else has thought of.

'I saw Jason that night at the fair, I went on a ride with him. She definitely left before him,' I lie. I am reminded of why we didn't hang out with these girls at school. Even with a rock-solid alibi Jason has already been convicted in the court of public opinion. I hope he's in the process of selling everything and moving away from here. I know it was the best thing I ever did. Once you get tagged with a label it becomes very hard to shake.

'So, are you married to anyone we might know?'

'No, no one from round here.' I pull up a photo of Chris on my phone – he always calls himself my trophy husband. Chris is surprisingly good-looking for such a kind man. He has no ego, no agenda, he's just really nice. It's one of the things that makes me so paranoid about losing him to another woman. He wouldn't have a clue if someone was putting the moves on him. He takes people at face value because that's how he is, no hidden secrets, no mendacious layers under the veneer. He is just a good guy. I smile as I look at his face. I miss him.

'Very cute,' Claire says with raised eyebrows. I can see she wants to say something else but she thinks better of it. In my mind I hear her asking what on earth he is doing with someone like me although that's probably not what she was going to say at all. I look at his face; it's a picture I took of him at the breakfast table. Nothing special about that day, he was just sitting with a piece of toast in his hand staring out of the window and I took the picture without him knowing. I often look at that picture and wonder what he was thinking. I was this wild crazy person when he met me, like a stray dog that he took in and looked after. My saviour, my protector. So many people in my life turned out to be someone different to who I thought they were, including myself. Not Chris though, never Chris.

I put my phone in my pocket and slip my shoes back on before standing up.

'It's been really great catching up, but I have to go into town,' I tell them. I have already got more information than I expected.

'Great to see you too,' Jenny and Claire say in unison, clearly pleased that I have decided to leave.

I wave a little and then make my way across the pebbles and back onto the concrete before going up the wooden steps to the gardens above. It's funny how everything seems smaller now that I am older. These stairs seemed never-ending when I was younger, like a ladder to the sky, which was obviously why it was called Jacob's Ladder. Maybe it's because my home is in the vast expanse of The Lake District and this town, this county, is so full of nooks and crannys that it's hard to see further than a few hundred feet at any given time, unless you are looking straight out to sea.

The gardens are exactly as I remember. The small café busy as ever in these summer months. Throughout the gardens are hidden benches and there is one in particular I want to find. At school it was known as the kissing bench, because it was hidden.

I find the bench and sit on it. Names I don't recognise are carved into the wood on every available space. I wonder if it's even the same bench at all. It doesn't matter though, it doesn't matter that the names or even that the bench is different. This is the bench I had my first ever kiss on. It was a good kiss, messy and awkward but a fond memory nonetheless. I stroke the wood and feel the balance restoring inside me. I spent so long hating this place and the people here that I forget that it's just a place. It's just geography, nothing else. The things that made it bad were nothing to do with the trees, the coast, the pebbles on the beach, the shops or the houses. None of that was the reason I ran away. There are places I haven't been yet because I am afraid. It's not the places I fear though, it's the memories that come with them. Just being here in this garden proves how much I can hide from myself. If someone had asked me just last week what the gardens looked like I could have given an overall picture, but being here has brought my memory of it to life. I can almost hear the voices of people I knew in the past and when I close my eyes I am right back there, just before my whole life fell apart.

I move from the bench and walk out onto the clifftop terrace that looks out over the sea. I never did like heights. I place my hand on the rocks and move forward until my hips are pressed against the rocky wall, the jagged stone edges digging into me. I feel the cold stone against my fingers as I grip and lean forwards, stepping on one of the black box lights that illuminate the walls at night. I'm feeling dizzy as I look at the slimy green rocks below. The tide is out but in my mind I see the water crashing against the side of the cliff, a memory clawing to the surface. My mouth feels dry and I find myself leaning further over the side, a part of me wanting to hurtle myself to the ground below to stop this madness. I think about the dog tags and know that I am running out of ways to avoid the places I need to revisit the most, scared of who I may encounter there. The more I find out, the more I want to run again.

I snap back to the present when I hear a woman cry out and feel a hand on my dress, pulling me backwards. I let go of the wall and tumble backwards, relieved when my bottom hits the paved path.

'Are you all right, love?' she says to me, her wide eyes and flushed cheeks far too close to me. 'You looked like you was going over.'

'I was just looking at the waves,' I say unconvincingly, knowing that my face is ashen.

'Let me help you get to a bench or something.'

I get to my feet and smile, trying to look less out of sorts than I feel. Past the woman's head at the far end of the path I see someone looking at me, except they aren't looking, they are watching. I push past the lady who helped me and walk towards the figure. She calls out after me angrily but I just keep moving, my hip sore from the fall, the faintest limp slowing me down. The person is gone down the steps and around the corner before I can reach them. These labyrinthine gardens are hard to navigate if you don't know your way around. I reach one corner and see the person disappear just ahead of me out through the gate and across the road to the car park. I am almost at the exit; I lose sight of the figure so I run faster, ignoring the bruise on my rump. I rush out and onto the road. I am stopped by the screech of tyres braking just a split second before the car hits me; it stopped but not soon enough. I feel myself fly through the air and land on the tarmac. My head hurts and my vision is blurred. I see people rushing towards me; I try to sit up but I am winded. The woman driving the red Mini Cooper that just hit me is crying as she checks my head for blood. I know I'm not seriously hurt but I may be concussed. The first thing I think is how glad I am that I hadn't been drinking today; if I had died it would have got back to Chris and I promised him I would try to control myself.

I manage to sit up, and through the legs of the people fussing over me and checking that I am OK I can see a car pulling out of the car park. It's a brown car. I see it more clearly this time. I know that car. The dog tags, the car. It's all pointing to one irrefutable answer.

He's back, and he knows what I did.

Chapter Twenty-Seven

In my hotel room I try to call Chris but it goes to voicemail. I managed to get out of going to the hospital by agreeing to let the woman who hit me drop me back at the hotel. I insisted I was fine but now that I am here alone I can feel where the car hit me. I really want to talk to the children. I feel like if I don't do it now I may never get the chance again. I have places I need to go, places I can't avoid any longer. I let this place get the better of me, I let myself get the better of me. I have the news on, waiting for the local segment to start, waiting to see if they have identified the body they found in the woods.

Some story about an outbreak of food poisoning at the county show, another story about some business closures further south and finally a small segment on the body discovered in the woods. The police are looking for leads. They are still searching in the woods for Mandy Green. No information on the identification, just the news that the body had been there more than sixteen years, by the looks of it. Could it be Hannah? Were we all about to find out what had happened to her? I always suspected I knew but this wasn't the ending I was expecting.

Maybe it's not connected at all but how likely was that? How many killers are in this town?

At the moment I only know of one. Me.

Chapter Twenty-Eight

Then

She didn't know how to feel about Felicity coming over tonight. As they walked towards the house together, Jasmine regretted inviting her. She acted like a tool sometimes and Jasmine wished there was a way to control her, but there wasn't. Felicity's home life meant she was in permanent self-destruct mode. Jasmine hoped Tim was out tonight and that they didn't see him. She just wanted him to be only for her. Not to mention the fact that she didn't know what he was capable of, how far he would go.

Jasmine watched Felicity with fascination some-times as she wrapped the boys in their class around her finger. It wasn't about the way she looked or anything like that, it was something in her, like she was transmitting something invisible that drove them crazy. She was like catnip.

They went inside and the house was empty. She noticed the breakfast plates from earlier had been cleaned and put away. Tim must have done it while she was at school. Felicity kicked her shoes off and flopped on the bench. Jasmine sat next to her.

'I wish *my* parents would go away. I would throw such a killer party. Should we invite a bunch of people round?' Felicity asked.

'Tonight?'

'Or tomorrow. We've got the whole weekend.'

'I don't think that's a great idea,' Jasmine said, although she had to admit there might be safety in numbers. Having other people there might make things easier.

'It'll give you an excuse to get all dressed up.'

'What do I need to get dressed up for?'

'Oh Tim, thank you for coming to my party,' Felicity said, mimicking Jasmine too loudly before erupting in a giggle.

Jasmine slapped Felicity on the thigh and she yelped. Jasmine felt she deserved it; she had said it loudly, with the intention of Tim hearing. She was trying to embarrass her and it wouldn't be the first time.

'He's just a lodger, that's all. I don't even like him.'

'Sure you don't.' Felicity's eyes widened excitedly as she spoke.

'I don't!' Jasmine said in a voice a few octaves higher than absolutely necessary.

'Thanks for having me over, you have no idea how much I appreciate it. I think Mum and Dan are on the brink of splitting up.'

'Because of you?'

'Oh God no, she doesn't give a damn about that. He says things in front of her and she barely reacts. I like her so much better when she's single.'

'Do you think you'll ever get married? I look at my parents and I can't imagine being like them. They seem to always know what they are doing.'

'I'm definitely getting married, as soon as I can. I don't think I've got it in me to go to university or anything like that. I'd like to marry someone brilliant and live as far away from here as I can. I always fancied Scotland, find myself a rich man who wants a pretty wife.'

'You would really leave?'

'I see the kids that stay behind, they all end up the same, either selling dope at the school gates or in the same pub every single weekend until their livers finally pack up. I don't want that.'

'You think you could stay married to one man for ever ever?'

'If he was the right man. Not like the idiots my mother goes for. Someone sweet and considerate. Someone who looks after me.'

'What about kids?' Jasmine said.

'Sure, why not. I wouldn't have just one though, that's cruel. I hate being an only child. Don't you?'

'Sometimes. I guess.'

'Imagine having a big brother or someone to talk to when your parents were being unreasonable. Not *your* parents, obviously; your parents are perfect,' Felicity said as she stood up.

'No one's perfect,' Jasmine replied before grabbing her bag.

'Look, I basically want your life. Your parents are amazing and they clearly love each other. Who wouldn't want what you have? The amount of times I've wished we could switch places. You have no idea how lucky you are, Jazz. I would kill to be you.'

She went upstairs to get changed. Jasmine pulled out some black cropped jeans and a V-neck T-shirt. She didn't want Felicity to think she was dressing to impress, so she kept it low key. Felicity burst into her room a few moments later and stripped off. She wasn't as shy as Jasmine. If Jasmine didn't know better, she would say she was deliberately doing it in front of the window. She didn't want to have to compete with Felicity when it came to Tim's attention. She was a bit taller than her, and Jasmine felt like she had the edge when it came to anything boy-related.

Felicity put on a baggy maroon sweatshirt dress. She had cut the ribbing from the neck so that it hung off one shoulder and even though it wasn't fitted it was definitely sexy, and the contrast with her black hair and rosy cheeks made it even more so. Jasmine tried to put that out of her mind. She didn't know how Felicity could wear that sweater in this summer heat; her own thin T-shirt was already clinging to her damp skin.

They went downstairs and Felicity put some music on the stereo in the kitchen. She opened the French doors and then started to dance and jump around to the music. Jasmine had known her a long time and she had never done this before. She knew it was all for Tim's benefit. She didn't even know if Tim was in the guest house or not; his curtains were always closed, no matter what time of day it was. Felicity pulled a bottle of vodka out of her school bag.

'I took it from home, my mum won't give a shit. I'll just stick it back filled with water. Get me a Coke or something, would you?'

'What are you doing?' Jasmine asked, smiling,

looking over to the guest house and hoping that Tim wouldn't come out. Jasmine got a bottle of Coke from the fridge and poured out two glasses, then Felicity filled them to the top with vodka. Felicity went out onto the deck and sat at the table. Jasmine brought the vodkas out and sat with her. Jasmine took a sip; the vodka was so strong she couldn't help but wince a little. It wasn't refreshing. Jasmine couldn't relax because she had a bad feeling about Felicity being there. Something bad was going to happen tonight, she could tell. Jasmine was so angry at herself for inviting her round now. Her parents had said they didn't want her to be alone all weekend, but she couldn't have gone to Felicity's. The atmosphere there was always so tense and the place reeked of cigarettes and booze. Not that Jasmine was precious or anything, but it was more comfortable here.

The door to the guest house opened and Tim leaned against the frame, holding a bottle of beer. He looked Felicity up and down before lifting the bottle up and wrapping his lips around the end. Jasmine hoped the sound of her breath catching wasn't as audible as it felt. The butterflies in her stomach thrashed, indiscernible from nerves. The feeling of uneasiness she felt around him was amplified in Felicity's presence. He squinted as he walked over to them and placed his beer on the table. He barely looked at Jasmine, and she saw his eyes flit across Felicity's exposed shoulder. There was something peculiar about the way he reacted to Felicity being there. She felt complicit in it, as though she had brought her friend for him to play with. She observed the way he looked at Felicity, the same way a cat looks at a small defenceless bird. Is that what she had done? Why hadn't she told Felicity about what happened at the fair? Why hadn't she told her what she suspected Tim had done? She should have told her parents, too. They never should have left her alone with him and she never should have put Felicity in harm's way. Why did she bring her here? She felt sick.

Tim sat with them; he was laughing at the lame anecdotes that Felicity was telling them. Jasmine didn't think half of them were true, but she smiled and nodded anyway. Occasionally Tim glanced over to Jasmine and the look on his face was so strange that she couldn't tell what it meant. His smile dropped and he looked almost sad for just a split second before he started laughing at something Felicity did again. The nausea in Jasmine's stomach was not helped by the vodka, but she didn't want to be completely sober right now as she watched what was unfolding in front of her.

The more she drank, the more resentful she felt. Maybe the fact that she was afraid of Tim made him more appealing to her; her fear and attraction had somehow mutated into one, almost dependent on each other. She knew she was being melodramatic, but she wanted to run away and hide. In a way this felt like a show for her benefit, but what did Tim have to gain by getting with Felicity, apart from the obvious? In the back of her mind she couldn't help wondering why he had never behaved this way with her. Felicity wasn't prettier than her, she knew she wasn't. She just had something that Jasmine didn't, confidence maybe.

Tim's beer ran out and he went back to his little house to get another one. Felicity leaned back in her chair with a look of accomplishment on her face. Jasmine really wanted her to go home, but she was stuck for now. Jasmine knew that Felicity was only rebelling against her own situation, acting out to feel different, to feel like someone else. It was a recurring theme. It wasn't her fault; Jasmine had been to her house enough to know that she would probably feel the same way in Felicity's place.

The truth was, she was jealous. Over the last couple of weeks Jasmine and Tim had forged a special bond. Knowing that he might be a murderer, this worried Jasmine. She always wondered when she was reading her true crime books how these duos found each other, how they could meet and then know that they had a shared destiny, something huge that pulled them together, like a magnet. She could feel that magnetism from him and it scared her. Jasmine knew she had made too much of a point of saying she didn't fancy him at all, and she actually hadn't realised how much she did like him until she was in direct competition with her friend. She only had herself to blame for what was happening. Tim returned to the garden and he was holding a joint. Felicity looked excited at the prospect.

'You going to tell on me?' Tim said in Jasmine's direction, without actually looking at her.

'Not if you give me some.' She took a swig of her drink. She wanted to loosen up and be interesting; she wanted to be funny and stop thinking for just five seconds. Jasmine had never smoked pot before. She had smoked cigarettes but never a whole one.

'Well, all right.' Tim smiled at Jasmine this time and the heaviness she was feeling disappeared for a moment. His eyes were lighter than before, bluer somehow, and he had a crinkle in his brow. His smile was something else entirely; he had perfect teeth and somehow you saw every single one when he smiled, like a cartoon smile. When he wasn't smiling his lips were always slightly parted and you could see his clenched teeth underneath. The good thing about having Felicity there was that Tim was so distracted by her that Jasmine could just stare at him as much as she wanted to, and he didn't notice.

'Is that what you were doing when I saw you at the fair? Getting this?' Jasmine asked.

'You got me,' he said. She detected a hint of anger. Because she'd brought up the fair?

She leaned back on her chair and let her eyes wander over every inch of him that she could see. His skin glistened with the heat of the evening sun. His T-shirt hugged his torso and she could see his muscle definition underneath. She could also see the chain he wore around his neck going into his T-shirt and a pendant of some kind under the surface. It was still so warm and now her drink was too. Jasmine stood up and went inside to pour herself another vodka and Coke, but this time she put some ice in it. She needed to cool herself down and she felt like a third wheel anyway.

'You OK?' Tim asked. She turned around to find he was standing behind her.

'Do you always sneak around like that?'

'You have no idea,' he said with a hint of menace. This was the first time all evening Jasmine had felt like he was focused on her and it made her uncomfortable. She hunched forward a little to make her chest seem smaller. He swayed a little, leaning forward. She could feel his breath against her forehead. She glanced up and their eyes connected for a moment. She had never been very good at reading the opposite sex, her history with Mr Morrell had proved that, but looking at Tim right now, there was an anger in him that scared her, even when he was being nice.

He seemed surprised at the way she looked at him. He pulled back and looked down apologetically. Maybe he sensed her fear, or maybe it was something else, but he stepped away, the connection broken.

'Can I get you something?' she asked, eager for him to go back outside. There was a part of her that just wanted to be the wallflower.

'Just checking you're OK. Your parents will kill me if anything happens to you.' He reverted to the nice Tim he was in front of her parents, pretending to be someone he wasn't. She knew there was something else under there, though. Something inside him that he wanted to stay hidden; she had just seen a flicker of it.

'You're not the babysitter and I'm not a baby.'

'Hey, I didn't say that. Just pace yourself, OK? You're knocking that vodka back pretty quickly.'

'What do you think my parents would do if I told them you were getting me high in the garden?'

He thought for a moment and then before he spoke, he wet his lips with the tip of his tongue. 'I trust you not to say anything, just like I didn't say anything about you and that teacher the night of the fair.'

'Do you like Felicity?'

'She's funny. I like her fine.'

Jasmine wasn't sure what he meant, but yet again she felt awkward being alone with him and thought asking any more questions would seem strange. She wasn't drunk enough yet to be confrontational.

The cold drink was welcome, and Jasmine drank faster than before. They went back outside and Tim lit the joint, puffing on it before handing it to Jasmine. She started to cough instantly, and a big grin broke out on his face again.

'What? Did I do it wrong?' Jasmine asked coughing, embarrassed.

'It works better if you cough.' He took the joint from her and handed it straight to Felicity. He looked at Jasmine with concern as she continued to cough. She felt like such a child. She drank down the vodka and watched him draw on the joint again. The drunker she got the harder she found it to look away from his lips.

It was still warm outside as the light slowly faded. It was getting late and Jasmine could feel herself crossing some kind of boundary that her parents never even thought to set for her, but she did know it was there. She was guilty of betraying her parents' trust. She could see that Tim wasn't interested in her; his focus was almost entirely on Felicity and in some ways Jasmine was almost grateful because she would have no idea what to do if he did like her. She saw Felicity leaning forward, her long, slick, black hair pulled over one exposed shoulder, and even Jasmine could see how sexy she looked. Tim took a long draw from the joint and then leaned forward and locked lips with Felicity. She breathed the second-hand smoke in from his mouth and Jasmine was destroyed. She needed to get out of there because a tiny part of her wanted to cry. When Tim pulled away, he looked at Jasmine and she saw that he was nervous of her reaction to what he had just done, checking for her disapproval. Felicity sank back in her chair, oblivious to how much she had just hurt her friend. Jasmine didn't blame her, she blamed herself. As Felicity exhaled, smoke billowing from her lips, Jasmine stood up and went inside the house. She just had to accept it. She had to accept that he didn't think of her the way he thought of Felicity. But she didn't have to watch.

Chapter Twenty-Nine

Back in her room Jasmine let the tears come. She felt so utterly betrayed. Torn between her feelings of concern for Felicity's safety and anger that Tim would do this. She thought he was different in some way. The way he had been with her had been different, hadn't it? She looked at the spare mattress on the floor, which was empty. Felicity was still outside with him. She wanted to tell her to come to bed, but on the other hand she just wanted to be alone. Her head swirled a little from either the tiny amount of pot she had smoked or maybe the quarter bottle of vodka. Jasmine wasn't sure she wanted to listen to Felicity telling her how his lips felt. She lay on the bed and listened to them talking outside. It was mostly Felicity doing the talking but that stopped after a while and Jasmine looked outside. Felicity was straddling him on the reclining garden chair and kissing him. As though he knew Jasmine was looking, his eyes opened as they kissed and he looked upwards towards Jasmine's bedroom window, eyes locked on Jasmine just before he closed them again. As if he wanted her to watch, wanted her to see what he was doing. What game was he playing? She pulled the curtains closed and moved her pillow to the other end of the bed so she no longer had to listen. She couldn't bear the thought of hearing them having sex. Felicity had had sex with two people before, another thing she had over Jasmine. She dreaded speaking to Felicity again, knowing how obsessive she was, knowing she would talk about nothing else, knowing that she would have to pretend she was fine with it.

Over an hour passed before Felicity finally entered the room. She giggled and tripped before flopping on the mattress on the floor. Jasmine pretended to be asleep.

'Oh my God,' Felicity said, before squealing into the pillow. Jasmine tried to ignore her, but she pulled on her arm.

'What is it?' Jasmine snapped.

'I think I'm in love.'

'You met him like eight hours ago. You're not in love.'

'He's such a good kisser.'

Jasmine was glad Felicity couldn't see her face.

'Can we go to sleep? I'm tired and my head hurts. Tell me in the morning.'

'Are you angry with me?' Felicity said, obvious concern in her voice.

Felicity was many things but she wasn't mean; sometimes she just didn't think beyond what was going on in her own head.

'No, I just feel a bit like I got ditched, that's all. We were supposed to be hanging out together tonight.'

'Sorry. I should have thought.'

'I'm tired, Felicity. I don't really want to listen to any of your sex stories.'

'OK, I won't tell you then. But wow, Jazz. There's something really weird about him, right?' Felicity said with a breathless enthusiasm.

'What do you mean, weird?' Jasmine asked, now interested in what Felicity had to say.

'After you left, we kissed for a while, which was hot.'

'I thought you weren't going to tell me.'

'No, wait. So I tried to . . . do more . . . and he wasn't having it. Grabbed my wrist and told

221

me I shouldn't throw myself away like that. What does that even mean?'

'He said no?' Jasmine asked. That didn't fit with what she'd seen from the window.

'I swear to God. Then he gave me another beer and I'm almost certain I saw him crying. Maybe he was just super stoned or something but after that he got up and punched the wall then he went inside his little hut.'

'I think it's probably better if you don't stay tomorrow night,' Jasmine said, unsure what Tim's behaviour could mean. She knew she couldn't go through this again tomorrow.

'Are you kidding?'

'I'm not kidding. Now go to sleep.' Jasmine wished she could make her leave now. She was angry that she let any of this happen. She was thirsty, so she got up and left the room without explanation as Felicity called out after her. She walked into the kitchen, where Tim was standing at the sink washing the glasses they'd drank out of earlier. He was shirtless, and Jasmine's eyes flitted across his back to his tattoo before grabbing a glass off the draining board and leaning across him to get a large drink of water.

'I thought you went to sleep,' he said.

'I'm thirsty and I needed to lock up. Wouldn't want anyone breaking in and killing me in my sleep.' It occurred to Jasmine that she was more annoyed with Tim than she was with Felicity. Why couldn't it be Jasmine? Why was it never her? She thought maybe she was disappointed that he was lured into Felicity's trap. Maybe she would think more of him if he had even resisted slightly. Her preconceptions about the person he was had faded and all she saw was another man trying to get off. But then she remembered seeing them on the lounger and the way he'd looked up at her. Was he trying to make her jealous? Is that why he wouldn't sleep with Felicity?

'You had better get going. I need to lock the doors,' Jasmine said sharply, unwilling to play his game.

'Have I upset you?' he asked, clearly knowing the answer already.

'What would I be upset about?' she said as she stared at him. He seemed to be full of regret. Up until now he had given her a wide berth, but she thought he knew he had made her feel bad. Maybe that was his intention all along. For the first time he shifted his gaze first, as though he could no longer stand her disapproval.

'You know, you're only sixteen. That's a problem.'

'You think a lot of yourself, don't you?'

'You think I don't notice the way you look at

223

me? I'm flattered but it's never going to happen. You're just a kid.'

'Felicity's the same age as me.'

'That's different. You wouldn't understand.'

'You know if I told my parents what you did tonight, they would throw you out. You aren't the person they think you are.'

'Are you the person they think you are?' The way he said it sounded like an insult, as though he had seen some darkness inside her that she wasn't aware of yet.

'Can you get out of the house now? I want to lock the door.'

Jasmine hated him for tonight but still felt this strange connection to him. He talked to her like she was the only person in the world. She saw a different side to him now, different to the way he behaved with Felicity earlier, more honest. Jasmine's expression was stone cold and he decided against challenging her and turned to leave the kitchen. This time she looked at the tattoo on his back closely. It was a dagger with some kind of inscription on it, though she couldn't quite read it.

He turned back to her and grabbed her wrist. 'We've all got different sides to us, we've all got secrets, Jasmine. You think your parents don't have secrets from you? You're wrong. Do you even know where they are this weekend? Do you know what they are doing?' he hissed.

'You're hurting me!' She pulled at her wrist and he let go.

He snatched his T-shirt off the lawn and walked back into the guest house. She locked the house. She considered telling her parents what he had done tonight, knowing they would get rid of him. She wouldn't do that though, not yet. There were still so many questions and she needed the answers. Maybe he would open up to her or maybe he would make a mistake. She couldn't have him just go and never get the answers.

Jasmine went back upstairs with her water and got back into bed. Felicity was asleep already; she'd drunk more than Jasmine, always did. Jasmine lay back and closed her eyes. She saw herself straddled across Tim, those blue eyes drilling into her as she moved slowly forward, kissing that perfect mouth of his. Why was he watching her when he was with Felicity? What exactly was it he was trying to do? Chess had never been a game she had played very well. Her father had tried to teach her time and again but she had always found it quite tedious. This reminded her of those lessons. Frank had always told her to think two moves ahead and focus on the endgame.

Chapter Thirty

When Jasmine woke up the next morning, Felicity was already dressed with her bag packed. Jasmine felt annoyed that this was probably going to come between them.

'Why didn't you tell me that you liked him?' Felicity asked.

'It doesn't matter,' Jasmine said, happy to keep her friend in the dark about her suspicions. She was also a bit jealous if she was honest, but the overriding emotion was fear that she was putting her friend at risk. Whatever game Tim was playing, the rules kept changing and she didn't want anyone else to get hurt.

'I never would have got off with him if I had known.'

The truth was that every time Jasmine had expressed any interest in a boy it was less than twenty-four hours before Felicity had got her claws into him. As if they were made more desirable by Jasmine's affection. If she had told her she liked Tim, Felicity probably would have just got with him sooner.

'It's not that big a deal.'

'Are we going to fall out over this?' Felicity said, looking concerned.

'No. We're cool,' Jasmine lied.

'I promise you I was telling the truth when I said that we didn't have sex. I would have, but we didn't. He wouldn't go any further than kissing. When I tried to do anything else, he would move my hands.'

'Don't try and make me feel better about this. I'll be fine, Felicity.'

Felicity's phone buzzed and she looked at it.

'Mum's outside, I've got to go. I promise you all we did was kiss.'

Jasmine stood up and hugged her. She wasn't annoyed at her really; she was who she was. A car horn beeped and Felicity rolled her eyes and then left the room. Moments later she heard the front door close and Felicity was gone. Now Jasmine really was alone. She didn't feel like eating and so she just opened the window and lay back on the bed. The warm sticky air from outside filled her room. She put some music on and drifted back into an uneasy sleep.

It was almost lunchtime the next time she woke up. She still felt anxious and disappointed, but she was also a little hungry so she went down into the kitchen. There was no sign of Tim anywhere, which was a relief, but she could see that he had been up already. The garden was marked up and he had begun digging a hole for a resistance pool. After her dad's surgery, the doctor had told him that swimming would be a good way to stay fit. They didn't have room in the old garden for anything like this but at their new house there was space for a modest pool. There was a half-drunk glass of water resting on the garden wall so she knew he was around somewhere. Jasmine opened the fridge and looked at the contents; nothing really appealed to her so she grabbed an apple from the fruit bowl instead. There was a knock on the French doors and she looked up to see Tim standing outside, looking down at his feet. That familiar feeling washed over her like an uninvited wave. Something about the way he stood made her swallow hard. She didn't want to open the door, but she did anyway.

'What is it?' she said bluntly; she didn't really want to talk to him. She was still angry, still disappointed.

'Just checking that you're OK.'

'Felicity left if that's who you're looking for.'

'It isn't. I was looking for you.'

'Well, I'm fine; I don't need you to check up on me.'

'Your dad called and asked me to check in on you. He said he called the house earlier and you didn't answer.'

'He wouldn't have asked you to check on me if he knew what kind of guy you are,' Jasmine said, surprised by the words that came out of her mouth. She was never confrontational but there was something about his demeanour that she couldn't lie to. She could say what she liked to him. Especially now that she wasn't concerned with impressing him anymore.

'I'm not a bad person. You've got me all wrong,' he said with a heavy sigh.

'Why her? Why not me? You said you saw the way I look at you which makes me think you were trying to hurt my feelings.'

'I like you more than I like her,' he said, confusing her.

'What does that mean?'

'It means yesterday, with Felicity, didn't mean

anything. Is that all you want from me? A quick fumble in the garden?'

'Am I supposed to be grateful that you used my friend to get off?'

'We can do that if you want, Jasmine. A quick one and done. Is that what you want?'

He moved in closer and she tilted her head back a little, the gap between them closing. She felt so small when he was close to her.

'No.'

She thought about what he'd said. Had he just said what she wanted to hear? Was he telling her he wanted more from her? The idea was both exciting and terrifying – he was almost ten years older than her. What could he possibly see in her?

'I'm sorry about Felicity; I was trying to put you off, if I am honest. I thought maybe I could make you hate me. I didn't sleep so well last night thinking I had hurt you. You didn't deserve that.' His voice was soft and low, and she knew he was lying. Whatever his motivation for kissing Felicity, he wasn't telling her the truth.

'Why would you try to make me hate you?'

'Because you're sixteen and I'm not that person. When I moved here, I didn't expect you to be like this. I didn't expect to like you as much as I do. I can't be that person. I thought if I could put you off, make you think I was interested in your friend, then this thing that we have, this connection that just seems to get stronger, would go away. It didn't work though because I can't stop thinking about you, about being with you.'

'OK. I understand,' she said; she thought she did understand what he was saying. He had used Felicity to make her hate him, but it hadn't worked, it had only made her feelings for him even stronger. The thought of him with someone else had pushed her desire to the surface. She couldn't deny it anymore. Not even her fear of who he might be could keep her from wanting him.

'I felt like we could be friends,' he said. He looked so serious and his eyes were totally locked on hers. Her anger dissipated and she forgot what she was ever annoyed about. She couldn't tell if he was playing with her or not. She was confused. As she pulled her eyes away, he did that thing where he wet his lips and Jasmine was right back where she was yesterday before Felicity came over. All was forgiven. Tim leaned down and pressed his lips to hers. He smelled of soap and his lips were wetter than she expected. She was dizzy and light-headed. He pushed his tongue inside her mouth, and she could taste a hint of coffee mixed with toothpaste. Time slowed and he put his arms around her waist, pulling her towards him. She kissed him back, taking his bottom lip in her mouth before pushing up on her tip toes and pressing her tongue into his mouth. Suddenly, he pushed her away and placed both of his hands on the doorframe to steady himself, his eyes closed as he buried his face in the pit of his elbow, as if trying to calm himself down.

'Where did you learn to kiss like that?'

Jasmine had kissed exactly seven people before that moment. None of them felt like this.

He brushed her hair away from her face again and moved towards her again, kissing her neck. She had goosebumps. Was this really happening? His fingers cupped the back of her neck and her skin was full of electricity. She moved in closer so that he was leaning over her; the weight of his body pressed against her turned her legs to jelly. He was so gentle, so tentative, that it put all thoughts of danger from her mind. She didn't feel threatened; she knew if she told him to stop that he would immediately. Maybe she had judged him too harshly. Maybe he had nothing to do with the death of her teacher. But if he had, he had done it for her, so that she would feel safe. She pushed all thoughts of Mr Morrell from her mind as she fell deeper under Tim's spell.

Chapter Thirty-One

Now

I have been sitting in front of the television for hours. I ordered room service and ate my way through two sharing platters. I didn't want to drink. I wanted to keep my wits about me in case I need to drive again. I can't fall apart in case I need to be in control. The past is catching up with me and when it finally hits I want to be ready. It's dark outside and I can feel the sea calling to me. The infinite blackness I want to submerge myself in. It's cloudy outside so there isn't even the reflection of the moon on the water. There's just beach and then a complete void. I wonder what it would feel like to just walk towards it and keep going. I wouldn't have to think any more, I wouldn't have this feeling of impending doom plaguing my every breath.

I have thought about death many times since that summer, not just my own. I stroke the back of my phone, wondering if maybe it's set to vibrate and I just haven't heard it ringing. Meeting Chris saved my life – before him I thought I had a different destiny altogether. I didn't think there was any good in me at all. When Daisy was born she was so pretty, so delicate and perfect with her little rosebud mouth and stormy blue eyes. I knew as soon as I saw her that if I was evil then someone so perfect couldn't have come from me.

I check the screen and see that I have called him six times now without him returning the call. It's obvious now that he is avoiding me, that he is upset that I left. I haven't spoken to him in several days. I can't blame him. In a way this trip has been a long time coming, not just for our marriage but also for me to be able to put a lid on the past.

I have fallen in love twice in my life. One was brief, and the other I have sabotaged from the moment it began. Falling for Chris was something I neither invited nor welcomed. He was so innocent and sweet, instantly trustworthy. I barely noticed myself falling in love with Chris. If I had noticed, I would have put a stop to it, but by the time I did it was too late; Daisy was almost with us and I was crazy about him. I had naively assumed in those first few months together that love conquers everything – until the reality of day-to-day life kicks in, that is.

The news comes on again. The body in the woods is of a man in his twenties. They don't say his name but I know it. The end of a story, a full stop.

Another piece of the puzzle falling into place, changing the picture completely. If he's been under the earth in the woods all this time then who has been following me? Whose car have I been seeing? The fear that I am losing my mind is manifesting into a reality. Am I seeing things? Can I even trust my own eyes anymore?

Why him?

He was such a brief part of my life and yet the ripples of his presence continue to affect me and throw everything I think I know into disarray.

When someone disappears without explanation it's hard to move on. I was the one who disappeared though. I was the one who didn't look back. There are two more places I need to go before I have the answers I am looking for. I should go now, I should have gone yesterday. Maybe I never should have left at all. Even with everything he did, he didn't deserve this.

I pick up the phone and call my husband, both frustrated and sad that he won't take my calls.

Daisy answers. 'What?'

'Oh, hi, darling. Where's your dad?'

'He's driving, he can't talk right now,' she says, but I can hear the TV in the background, telling me they are at home. Conspiring.

'I just wanted to know how you are all doing?' I ask. I could call them out on their lie but I hardly have a leg to stand on.

'Really good. When are you back?'

'I thought you guys were coming down here?'

'Dad's not sure now, he might have to work.'

I try not to sound relieved. 'I'll be back in a few days. Sorry I left at such a bad time.'

'It's fine, Mum,' Daisy says in an effort to get me off the phone. I don't have the energy for a conversation like this right now. I wonder if I wouldn't have preferred it if the phone had stayed unanswered. I feel like a terrible wife and mother, but at least I called.

'OK, I'll speak to you soon. Love you all.'

'Bye.'

The phone goes dead and I am glad. I shouldn't be, but I am.

I pull out my laptop and start looking at names, names that pop into my head, people I might remember, names from the news reports that seem familiar, anything I can find. There are a handful of names I don't enter, knowing full well that I will find nothing, including my own. Chris, who is all about the wonders of technology, is surprised by my lack of interest in any kind of social media. He doesn't realise the thought of getting a message from someone I used to know, anyone I used to know, literally gives me chills.

I have more questions than answers now, even though the answers linger somewhere in my mind, trapped in my memory. I have most of the information now but I am still missing something, I know I am. There is something staring me straight in the face and I can't see it. I've been chasing a ghost; now that I know he isn't in play I can move past him. Someone is out there trying to make me think I am going mad. I instantly feel more focused. I will find out the truth.

Chapter Thirty-Two

Then

Something had disturbed Jasmine in her sleep. When she woke up it was dark and there was a welcome chill in the air, the smell of a coming rain. She still had her window open and was lying on top of the covers. She looked to the right-hand side of the bed; it was empty – it hadn't been when she'd fallen asleep. The faintest smell of Tim lingered on her pillow but he wasn't there. A part of her wanted to message Felicity and tell her what had happened, but she knew it wasn't the right time, and that Felicity wasn't the right person. She had thought she would feel completely different but the only thing she felt was guilt. She looked outside to see if he had gone back to the guest house. The front door was slightly open but the lights were off.

She got out of bed, holding her breath. She opened the door a sliver and saw a dim light coming from her parents' bedroom. The light moved and she could tell it was a torch. Either there was an intruder in her house, or something that she couldn't bring herself to contemplate was happening in the room next door. The drawers opened and she heard papers moving around in them, rustling as though he was searching for something. Maybe there was an innocent explanation for what he was doing, but she couldn't think of one.

She crept into the hallway and pressed herself against the wall, slowly angling her head enough to look inside her parents' room. Tim was going through all of their drawers. He pulled open Lisa's underwear drawer and rooted through it; he pulled out a bra and held it to his nose for a few moments, breathing it in, before stuffing it in his pocket. He moved to the other side of the room and Jasmine heard her parents' wardrobe door open. She decided she needed to do something. She sneaked back to her room and made a little noise, turning her bedroom light on so that it spilled into the hallway, to alert him that she was awake. She was reminded that she didn't really know him at all, neither did her parents. She couldn't help but feel cross with them. They'd had a few lodgers over the years but they had never let anyone get this close before, never trusted anyone to be alone with her. He was very good at manipulating people to do what he wanted. She thought back to the previous night, with Felicity and the way he had made sure Jasmine had been watching, making her jealous to make her acknowledge her feelings for him, ignite that jealousy within her. Maybe it was never about her at all. Much easier to look through the house when you are already inside and what better way to for him to get inside the house than to manipulate Jasmine into letting him sleep there. How had he hoodwinked them all into trusting him? What was it he was looking for?

She walked quickly to the bathroom and locked the door. Her heart was thumping. Her phone was in her bedroom and she was furious with herself. What if he decided to break the bathroom door down? Why would he? She had already given him anything he might want to take. She flushed the toilet even though she hadn't been. She waited until she could hear no noise, hoping that the sound of her moving about in the night might have scared him away. She imagined him standing outside the bathroom door, waiting for her to emerge so he could hurt her. Finally, she pulled together enough courage to unlock the door. When she went back into her room, she could sense that he had gone from the house.

She went to close her bedroom window because the temperature had dropped and the rain was coming down. She was shaking and not just because she was cold, she had been a fool, letting her guard down, believing he thought she was special.

As she looked out she saw Tim crossing the garden back towards the guest house. She ducked out of the way and waited a few moments before looking again. He was standing there looking up at her window. His eyes snapped to hers in an instant and she felt her blood run cold. He didn't react to the rain pouring down his face. Jasmine didn't feel excited. She felt terror. He smiled at her, that big wide unnatural grin; although it was dark she could see his face clearly. *Was this really happening?*

He finally turned away and went inside. Jasmine's eyes were transfixed on the guest house door. What if he came back? Maybe she had enough time to run and get a knife before he could get to her. *What was he doing in her parents' room? What did he want?* Jasmine thought back to this morning when he'd kissed her, and it occurred to her it only happened after she threatened to tell her parents about what happened with Felicity. Was he trying to keep her from saying anything by giving her what she thought she wanted? Ten out of ten for distraction. The light inside the guest house went off and she kept watching. If he came out again, she could call the police at least before he could get to her. She felt so stupid, so alone, so completely vulnerable. Who the hell was he?

Chapter Thirty-Three

Now

The body is definitely Tim's. I thought he had breezed out of town the same way he came in, but in truth he'd never left.

The police are treating the death as suspicious, which goes without saying, as he couldn't have buried himself in the woods. The national press have started to turn up; things are getting exciting around here. Any café I walk into, it's all anyone is talking about. So far, a few stories have emerged about him in the newspaper, things I had heard before and some things I hadn't. He was full of secrets, anyone with eyes could tell that. The local people who remembered him said he was homeless but I knew that wasn't true. Anyone he truly interacted with was either dead or gone, like me. Now would be the time for me to go to the police and tell them what I know, but I am still not sure *what* I know. I know that Tim had a brown car, the same brown car I thought I saw on the road just the other night, unless I was just imagining it. Maybe I was seeing what I wanted to see. Did I know all this time he was dead? I need to start picking at those scabs again, I need to set the past free so that I can get away from it. Even if I end up in prison, I don't care anymore. It's no less than I deserve after what I have done. I still don't have all the pieces and I need to know before I speak to the police.

As I go to leave the hotel room I notice a piece of paper has been pushed under my door. I stare at it for a moment before opening the door and looking into the hallway. The paper wasn't there before I put my make-up on, so it definitely hasn't been there long. I open it. The words appear in an unsteady scrawl.

I KNEW YOU WOULD COME

I fold the paper and put it aside. I look at the minibar and consider taking a drink or two to steady myself before I leave the hotel but think better of it. I go to the window to try to see the person who left the note. There are a couple of people walking along the front, but they are too far away to make out. Grabbing my bag, I rush out of the room, down into the lobby and outside. Unsure what I am looking for. Who I am looking for.

Why would they reach out to me like this? How could they know I would come? I had to think. This confirms that I have missed something, that there is something I should know but I don't. Something that links me to Mandy Green, something that would make me come back when she disappeared. I need to find out more about Mandy.

I start to run along the sea front, looking at every face as I do. I don't recognise anyone. Over the years one of my greatest fears was running into him again – to think that he was dead all that time. I thought he had just left town. So many times I have wondered where he went, who else's lives he'd turned upside down, when all the time he was stuck here.

I reach the centre of the beachfront. I can go into town or I can keep going to the end. I have been avoiding that part of the beach more than any other. It seems more secluded somehow, more dangerous.

I knew Hannah Torrence, I even saw her the night she disappeared. I didn't know anything about Mandy Green though. Maybe people her own age might be able to tell me more. I need to see if I can find anyone who knew her. Knowing what this place is like, I expect the places kids hang out are all the same as before. We used to sneak out and go to Blackmore Gardens when I lived here. The gardens run alongside the bowling lawns and between the town and the library. The chances of me finding anyone who knew Mandy there are as good as any. I walk up through town and then through the cemetery into the gardens to check all my old haunts. This town probably has more memorial benches than actual people. You are never stuck for a place to sit. I see a group of teens messing about inside the large shelter and so I approach them. It's two girls and three boys. They are passing a vape cigarette around and I can smell candy floss.

'Hello,' I say, sounding more posh and grown-up than I ever thought I could.

The boy hides the vape behind his back. 'Hello?'

'I'm just wondering if any of you guys knew Mandy Green?'

All eyes dart to one of the girls in the group.

'Allie knew her, didn't you, Al?' the boy says immediately.

'Hi, Allie. Can you tell me anything about Mandy?'

Allie looks down at her hands, clearly uncomfortable. The whole mood inside the shelter has changed.

'We were mates. We were hanging out in town and I guess I ditched her. We had an argument and she stormed off. No one's seen her since.'

'What did you argue about?'

'Me.' One of the other two boys in the shelter pipes up, looking both smug and apologetic at the same time, which is quite some feat.

'They broke up a while back, but she was still upset that I hooked up with him,' she said, embarrassed. The rest of the group were smirking but to their credit they were trying to hide it.

'Was Mandy the kind of person to just get in a car with a stranger?'

'I don't think so. She wasn't stupid. But it was pissing down that night, so maybe she did.'

'Have you ever seen an old brown Cortina in town? It's a real mess of a car, not the usual for these parts.'

'Once or twice, I think, maybe,' Allie said and her friends all nodded in agreement.

'Has it ever approached any of you?'

'Nah.'

'Has anything else like this ever happened, did anyone else ever go missing?'

'Don't think so.'

'And Mandy wasn't the kind of girl who would run away?'

'She was kind of messed up, I guess, but I don't think she would run away. She never ever talked about it or anything,' Allie said.

'Messed up how?'

'Same as everyone else. Family stuff.'

'Her mum works up the newsagent's, right? What about her dad?' I ask.

'She never knew him. Died before she was born. Her stepdad is in prison for dealing.'

'How did he die? Her real father.'

'Killed himself. Threw himself off a cliff or something.'

I feel goosebumps and my skin runs cold. I ask the question even though I already know the answer.

'Do you know what his name was?'

'No, but he was a teacher up at the school. Got fired for sleeping with one of the girls then he killed himself.'

This changed everything. Mandy going missing was clearly connected to the past, to that summer, to everything that happened. So, the person who took Hannah all those years ago got away with it and now they were doing it again. Why? Sixteen years is a long time to go without hurting someone, if that was your thing. I wanted to believe that I was seeing things where nothing was there but it was hard to deny that the one factor all of these things had in common was me.

I pull a twenty-pound note out of my pocket and hand it to Allie. I can see her clothes are worn and she doesn't really take care of herself. I wish someone had tried to make me value myself when I was her age, not that I would have listened.

'Thanks,' I reply, walking away. I hear them all swoop in on the girl who now has the money. At their age we would have found someone to buy some alcohol for us. I remember there was a guy who used to wait on the corner of the marketplace and he would buy alcohol for anyone who wanted, charging a two-pound fee for each purchase. He didn't do badly out of that work at all.

I feel a picture of the past forming in my head, like a book you read once and then when you watch the movie several years later, you know it's not exactly as you remember it, but you aren't sure what's different. It would be easy to find out; all I need to do is go back home. I'm not sure I'm ready.

Chapter Thirty-Four

Then

Jasmine had three large assignments to complete over the summer for her A Level interviews. The college had asked for a piece for each course she wanted to attend, as there was high demand for the ones she was interested in. She decided she wanted to focus on those rather than what had happened last night; she couldn't keep torturing herself by thinking about Tim and what they had done together. If she told her parents about him going through their room then she would have to admit what she had done with him, why he was even in the house at that time of night. She couldn't bear the thought of the look of disappointment they would give her.

They had been asked to fill a seventy-five-page scrap book, so she planned to use five pages for each country they had visited since she was in her mother's stomach. Her parents had put a world map up in their dining room, which filled almost a whole wall, and had flag stickers on all the countries they had visited, a few from before Jasmine was born. There was a slightly heavier concentration in central and South America, as her mother was fluent in Spanish and Portuguese and could get by with many of the local dialects.

She ran upstairs and rooted through her wardrobe. She was almost out of clean summer clothes. The small amount of rain last night had made little difference to the suffocating heat – she thought today might be the hottest day yet. She found an old pair of harem trousers and a halter-neck top. They didn't really match but she didn't care. She scooped her dirty clothes from the chair and the floor before taking them downstairs and throwing them in the washing machine. She turned the machine on and then went straight to the freezer to look for an ice lolly or something because it was so hot, she could barely think. There was a freeze pop in the bottom drawer and she laid it across the back of her neck to try and cool herself down.

The side gate to the garden opened and Tim

walked through holding a heavy-looking messenger bag which he put on the ground immediately as if to hide it from Jasmine. He looked surprised to see her in the kitchen but came to the door anyway. She hadn't seen him since he'd looked up at her from the garden in the pouring rain; they hadn't spoken since he'd whispered words of affection into her ears as they lay on her bed. Was he even going to try and explain himself?

He opened the door and stepped inside, looking through to the back of the house, presumably to check that she was alone. She had noticed he did that a lot. She was afraid to smile or be nice or anything. Which Tim was this?

'How is your day going?' he asked, his eyes boring into her, almost daring her to challenge him on what she had seen.

'Felicity was asking after you. She's got it bad,' Jasmine said, partly to see how he reacted to the information and partly to make sure he knew she didn't want to play his game.

'Did you tell her? About us?' he said, acknowledging what had happened between them. Was he just going to pretend that she hadn't seen him in her parents' bedroom? That wasn't a dream, she knew it happened, and yet the way he was acting said otherwise. Either she was crazy or he was a very good liar.

'No. I don't want to make her feel bad.'

'She didn't mind making you feel bad.'

'That's on her. Where have you been?' Jasmine nodded towards the bag on the ground.

He didn't move his gaze once from her eyes and she found herself inhaling, preparing for a period of less air. She remembered kissing him and how it felt to have his lips on hers. He leaned towards her, stepping forward at the same time so she had no choice but to step back and rest her hands against the dining table. Standing so close to Jasmine, her only option was to lean right back and stare up at him. He didn't kiss her immediately. She watched as the blues of his eyes moved slowly across her face. When his gaze finally reached her mouth, he moved towards her, his hot breath reaching her lips long before she felt his soft, wet lips on hers. She wanted to push him away but there was nowhere to go. Her heart thumped as she let it happen, scared to tell him no, hoping this would be enough.

She ran her hand along his forearm, She felt the veins and the downy hair on his skin. He pulled away, hovering close to her face, looking straight at her with his glistening mouth just millimetres away from hers. Was this all about making her want him? She hated that it was working. Her hand on his arm trailed down to his wrist and her fingers brushed against the knotted braid.

'Where did you get that friendship band from?' she asked, surprising herself.

His smile faded immediately.

'A good friend of mine gave it to me.'

'A woman?'

'Yes.'

'Where is she now?'

He thumbed the knotted band gently, a softness creeping across his face, an expression she didn't recognise. He had so many faces, she wondered if she had even seen the real one.

He looked at her again, all trace of sentimentality gone, a storm raging behind his eyes.

'She's dead,' he replied.

The way he said it petrified her. He had never uttered two more loaded words in their time together. His statement felt like a warning, or maybe even a threat.

The sound of her parents' car crunching on the gravel outside startled her. They would walk in at any moment. She had to decide right now if she was going to tell them what she had seen him doing in their room. Telling them that would lead to a whole load of other questions that could put her relationship with them at risk – it might change what they thought of her, what they thought about what happened with Mr Morrell. She couldn't tell them. She was close to Tim now; she could try and play him at his own game. She thought about her mother at her own age and wondered what secrets she had kept from her parents, whether she'd ever done anything like this.

'Sorry,' Jasmine muttered.

'I need to go. I've got things to do.' He pulled away from her and left, grabbing his bag from outside the kitchen door and walking into the guest house without looking back.

Chapter Thirty-Five

Sitting at the dinner table with her parents was hard for Jasmine. She felt as if she was lying to them all the time, because she was. Her biggest fear was that she would tell them that she'd seen Tim rifling through their belongings and they wouldn't believe her. She knew full well how manipulative Tim was. If they asked, he could tell them anything. She suspected, maybe unfairly, that they had their doubts about what happened with Mr Morrell. There were lots of carefully crafted questions at the time about how much she may or may not have led him on. She knew other people had accused her of being the instigator of the incident, even with the video evidence. She didn't think it would be a total leap for her parents

261

to imagine she might have been less innocent than she had claimed to be.

The silence at the dinner table had become unbearable and so Jasmine grasped for something to say to fill the void.

'I have lots of washing to do, I'm out of summer clothes. It's been so hot,' she said.

'I'll put a load in after dinner. How are you feeling? You're very quiet.'

'Just a lot going on at the moment, you know?'

Lisa jumped on the opening. 'I didn't realise you were friends with the Torrence girl. You've never mentioned her before.'

'I don't mention a lot of people,' Jasmine said, trying not to sound snippy.

'How did you know her?'

'Just from around. I heard some talk about the vigil. The police say the evidence points to Mr Morrell. He did it and now he's gone and they have no idea what he did with her body.'

'What else have you heard?'

'Just the usual crap. People found out about him coming after me at the fair. Some people said it should have been me, that I was the one he wanted to take and not Hannah. They are saying it like it's my fault she's missing.'

'What happened to her wasn't your fault, darling,' Frank said. 'That creep was always going to do something crazy like that. He's got form. Would you rather it was you?'

'Of course not.'

'Thank goodness Tim was there. That was some luck. He's like your guardian angel.' Her mother smiled, resting her knife and fork on the plate to indicate she was done.

'Your mother and I finish work early on Friday. We thought maybe we could do a trip to the Indian restaurant and then go to the cinema together or something. We haven't done that in a while.'

'Maybe, I don't know, I'd like to go to the vigil,' Jasmine said, before excusing herself from the table. She knew her parents would chalk it down to fallout from Mr Morrell's suicide and she was happy for them to think that for once.

Jasmine had barely touched her dinner – it was too warm to eat anyway – and so she took her plate to the bin and scraped the remnants away. She went back into the dining room to work on her geography project as a distraction from Tim, from her parents.

The powerlessness of her situation was making her crazy. She pulled out the photo albums from their trip last year to Nicaragua. She had fond memories of the place. The landscape was staggering; it had felt almost prehistoric, a far cry from their quaint little house in their model village of a town. She started to go through the photos, the volcanic scenery making her nostalgic for a country she would probably never go back to. They had never been to the same place twice. She saw faces of people she had become close to and then, after they left, lost touch with entirely. She couldn't imagine doing anything differently, but it occurred to her that they existed within this tiny snapshot of happiness and when they left everything likely went back to the way it was before. Were they really changing anything?

Jasmine placed the pictures she had selected for Nicaragua face down on the scanner one by one and pressed copy. When she was done, she put the original photos back in the albums and returned the albums to the shelves. She sat and wrote an account of her stay there, leaving the space between photos on the first page blank for the country status which she would draw up nicely. Over six million inhabitants and a GDP of almost fourteen billion dollars. It was late and her shoulders ached from hunching over on the floor. She placed her copies inside the scrap book, ready to stick them down later when she had drawn her stats chart.

She got a drink from the kitchen and then went back into the dining room and grabbed some more of the photo albums to go through them. She noticed how young she looked in the pictures and realised how recent that was; she had been fourteen – almost fifteen – years old. The girl she was in those pictures was playing with the other children. She felt so much older than that now.

The albums for Honduras were next. They had visited when Jasmine was thirteen years old and built wells in several villages, as there was a severe lack of clean drinking water. She wrote a paragraph on how the country made a lot of money from mining but unfortunately the metal leaked into the water, making a lot of it undrinkable.

She had made a good friend in Honduras, Maria, who still wrote to Jasmine sometimes. Her older sister had gone missing and the police had never found her, although Maria didn't think they'd looked very hard. Crime in Honduras was a huge problem and it had the more homicides than almost any other country on the planet. She decided to use the Marcus Aurelius quote that her dad had told her once – 'Poverty is the mother of all crime' – but it didn't feel right to talk about Maria's sister in her homework. Once she had chosen her pictures of her time in Honduras, she decided to move to another room; it was a bit stuffy in the dining room. She took the next set of albums into the kitchen, wishing it wasn't so warm. It was approaching midnight and her parents were in bed, but she was buzzing and she knew she wouldn't sleep. She grabbed a bottle of coconut water from the fridge and sat down to her albums. She hadn't noticed before, but Tim was outside in the dark, digging the hole for the swimming pool. Every day when she looked out there the hole got bigger but she never saw him actually working on it – now she knew why. Seeing him digging in the dark like this was like watching him dig a grave. It would be big enough to fit all three of them in. She shook off the thought – it was ridiculous, she was being melodramatic. She had no proof he was a killer.

The Cambodian albums took a lot longer than anticipated because she couldn't concentrate. Tim was shirtless because of the heat and she found herself staring at the tattoo on his hip that was illuminated by the soft solar lighting in the garden. It was a black rose with the words *forever yours* wrapped around it. She shrank as she remembered being with him, embarrassed that she had let him so close. There was also the dagger on his back. There was another tattoo on the top of his arm that she hadn't noticed before. It looked like a pair of guns crossed over with the letter S over the top of them. If she wanted to get rid of him she had to have proof that he really was bad. She couldn't let him suspect that she was turning the tables on him.

She poured an ice-cold glass of orange juice and took a sip before going outside.

'Good evening,' she said, holding out the drink.

He took the glass and she watched him drink, throwing his head back until every last drop was gone. Her eyes wandered down his neck, his chest, his stomach and then on to his tattoo. She wondered who he'd got that for. Was it the girl who gave him the friendship band he wore on his wrist? The dead girl.

'I didn't wake you, did I?'

'No, I was up anyway. I wondered when you were digging that hole.'

'Too hot in the day for that kind of work.'

'Kind of creepy doing it at night though.'

'Hadn't you better get to bed?' he said, handing her back the glass. 'I have to get on with this.'

'Not really tired. I find it hard to sleep in this heat. I've got some work to do anyway,' Jasmine said before going inside and locking the door behind her, making sure he noticed her doing it. She grabbed her books and headed back into the dining room to work through the night. She looked back to the garden to check he had stayed there. She wanted him to know that she wasn't afraid of him; the truth was that there was still this

267

conflicting feeling within her. There was something wrong with him, there was no doubt about that. One thing was for certain: he had a plan, something he was working towards. Maybe she was part of it or maybe she was just in his way. One way or another she was going to find out what he was doing there.

Chapter Thirty-Six

Jasmine didn't particularly remember much from the first few countries they'd visited; she was too young and spent most of the time either on a sling strapped to her mum or being cared for by elderly women not strong enough to do the physical work. Her dad loved to regale her with stories of their travels, particularly of the many embarrassing things she had done on those trips. Her parents had given her a cheap little handheld camera when she was really young so she could document things for herself. She still had the pictures somewhere.

The next country on the list was Belize. She decided to take a break and see if Tim was still digging the garden. She went outside but he wasn't there. The shovel was abandoned on the ground and it looked like he hadn't got much further than when she'd left him out there a couple of hours ago. She wondered if he was in the guest house. She could go in under the pretence of making sure he was OK, under the pretence of wanting to be alone with him again. Her hand hovered over the handle and she considered what the worst that could happen was. She realised she had no idea what that might be.

'What are you doing?' Tim said. She turned to see him walking out of the kitchen, brows furrowed. 'Did you go inside?' he asked, his face awash with rage.

'Where were you just now?' she said, realising that he had been in the house, but she hadn't seen him. How did he get inside when she had locked the doors earlier? To get from the dining room to the garden she had passed every room on the ground floor and he hadn't been in any of them. The frown disappeared from his face and his eyes turned kind, but she didn't believe them.

'I was looking for you,' he said, but she knew he was lying; he was somewhere else in the house. What was he doing?

Pushing past him, she went back into the house, closing the French doors behind her. What was in the guest house that he was so worried about her seeing? She had seen the look on his face when he thought she had gone inside. Maybe the key to whatever game he was playing was in there.

When looking through the photo album for Belize, Jasmine was hit by how pretty it was. They had visited the island of San Pedro, which was so colourful and the people were so friendly, it had been the inspiration for *La Isla Bonita*, the Madonna song. Jasmine had been eleven and they had refurbished a medical centre, although in reality she did very little besides play football in the street with the kids of the neighbourhood. It was one of her fonder memories of travelling abroad. When she got to the final Belize album, she opened the sleeve and found a piece of fabric pressed between the pages, a bright blue piece of torn silk. Jasmine had no idea where it was from but it had been ironed flat from being squashed among the pages of the album for so long. She turned the pages and remembered Ladyville, where they had helped to paint a community centre where people could bring their children. Jasmine's mother was very artistic, and she had painted a brilliant mural of cartoon characters on the walls. When the work was finally completed there was a party to celebrate and officially open the place. The local press had been there, and her parents had posed front and centre for photos with their colleagues.

The next photo was of Jasmine and her mother. Lisa's face bore a glowing smile as she looked past the camera to the person taking the photo. Jasmine could tell by the look on her mother's face that it was Frank. She completely adored him. Then something in the background caught Jasmine's eye and she dropped the photo.

It couldn't be.

Overcome with a wave of nausea, Jasmine stared at the back of the picture that had landed face down, scared to pick it up and turn it over. But she did. And there, standing less than twenty feet behind her and her mother, at the makeshift bar, was a man staring straight into the camera with piercing blue eyes.

It was Tim.

Chapter Thirty-Seven

Now

More bones have been found in the woods. It's actually made the national news, a tiny segment but I watch greedily in the hopes of gleaning any more information. The concierge has brought me a selection of papers and I root through, looking for anything new, anything I haven't seen before. More police have been brought to the site for a more thorough search, and the subtle implication that the woods are a mass burial ground runs through the newspaper articles. The media excitement is palpable, as though they have forgotten these are real people they are talking about.

The papers have revealed the identity of the

man in the woods, confirmed by the dog tags found with the body. They have also accessed his bank records which show that all activities ceased sixteen years ago. Tim Fulton was in the woods all that time and I didn't know. Seeing the name sends a chill down my spine. The article in the *Echo* paints him as a homeless loner, a man who was dishonourably discharged from the army after being implicated in a murder investigation. He was exonerated but the damage was done and so he disappeared, many people still convinced that he was a killer.

None of this matches up with what little I knew. There's no photograph of his face but it's etched on my memory. The only picture is of the cordoned-off woods which are still being searched for evidence after the discovery of more human bones.

I don't know how I know, but I know it's Hannah.

It's all connected. That summer was the end for so many of us. I think about her mother and father and how I would see them walking around town asking questions after her disappearance. I wondered why they never asked any of the younger people what might have happened, as if we were unreliable in some way, or maybe we were just invisible. It was more real for us than they could ever know. We never knew why or how she disappeared; it was always a mystery. We never knew if whoever did it was coming for one of us next.

I decide to walk towards the woods, still feeling guilty from driving under the influence the other day. It's a long walk but I don't mind; I could use the time to think, to prepare myself for what happens next. It feels strange to be so sad about someone I only knew very briefly but I am, especially knowing he died when I was angry with him. I don't know why that makes me feel worse; it's not as if he knew or even cared what I might have been thinking after he was gone. As for Hannah, we said hello now and then, that was it, and yet I feel responsible, as though maybe I could have saved her if only I had tried. As I walk I think about what else they might find up there. Is the truth finally going to come out?

Almost every low garden wall I pass is made of pebbles or stones, adding to the fairytale feeling of this place. Apt, really, when I think of the grim goings-on. I try to remember how I used to feel about it, before I knew what I know. I thought it was the prettiest place imaginable. I have since realised that what we see is not always all there is. That applies to people as well as places.

I reach the theatre and consider turning back. Walking to the woods means I will be walking past the road my house was on. My mother may well still be there. I haven't spoken to her since the day I ran away and I have made no enquiries as to whether she is alive or dead. Like Shrödinger's cat, as long as I don't look, she is alive and crying into the sink where I left her. But I can't avoid it much longer. Maybe the woods were never my destination, maybe I always knew I would end up back at that house. I had hoped when I left that I would never see it again, but I have avoided it so consciously that it has become a magnet, always there, ready to receive me, pulling me to make me face the truth about myself. About what I did.

Chapter Thirty-Eight

Then

Jasmine was alone in the house. Tim could walk in at any moment. Who the hell was he? She went over every interaction they'd had since he arrived and it became clear he had always had some ulterior motive. Whenever she had questioned him or got in the way he would do something to make her forget. Like sleight of hand. She felt so conflicted about everything. She remembered how tender he had been when they were together, then just a few hours later he was ransacking her parents' room. She just wished she knew what it was he wanted. It certainly wasn't her. Her only advantage at the moment was that he probably thought she was still under his spell.

She looked out to the driveway; Tim's car was there. Her parents wouldn't be home for a few hours. She was going to talk to them as soon as she had proof. She needed to find out more before she presented her parents with the truth. Something he couldn't wheedle his way out of with that crocodile smile of his. If she found the right leverage maybe she could just make him leave without telling her parents at all. That was the ideal situation, then there was no danger that he would tell them she had slept with him. She didn't want to stay in the house alone until they got home. She picked up her phone and called Felicity.

'Can I come over?'

'Now? I guess. Warning though, Mum's off her face. Are you staying?'

'Probably not, I'll get my dad to pick me up after work. I'll walk over now.' Jasmine put the phone down before Felicity had a chance to protest.

She took the photograph from Belize out of her pocket and studied it again before quickly putting it in her jewellery box to hide it in the hidden tray under the ring compartment. She didn't want her parents to see it. They didn't deserve that, not after all the hospitality they had given Tim. They would be terrified, and she couldn't bear to imagine the look of disappointment on her father's face. What if he confronted Tim? Tim was much stronger than him, more menacing. In her father's condition he could get really hurt.

Her instinct that Tim was hiding something in his lodgings seemed completely legitimate now. Every time she got suspicious of him, he had put her off the scent. She knew now though. She knew he wasn't right. Could she even trust her own judgment anymore? She reminded herself that her parents also trusted him. This wasn't all on her. There was a spare key in the kitchen drawer, so the next time he was out she would go and investigate.

Felicity's mother Carol was in the kitchen, and the usual smell of nicotine and spilled alcohol wafted up Jasmine's nose as she entered the house. Felicity led Jasmine up to her room where she had been watching *Friends* relentlessly while sneaking sips of a bottle of cheap rum. She had been drinking for a while by the time Jasmine got there. They settled in and watched together. Felicity put her head on Jasmine's shoulder, the smell of rum emanating from her, her once full bottle now holding only two inches of the clear off-brand liquid.

'You never come over. To what do I owe the pleasure?'

'Just missed you. That's all.'

'What's going on with you? You've been pretty evasive lately.'

'Nice word.'

'Are you still upset with me about the other night? I was pretty blasted. I'm sorry. I think I knew you liked him. I don't mean to do things like that, Jazz, I just get a bit jealous of everything you've got. I wish I was more like you, you're my hero.'

'Don't be daft. It's OK.'

'Did he say anything about me?'

'No, sorry,' Jasmine said.

'You haven't ever talked to me about Mr Morrell. You can tell me the truth, you know,' Felicity slurred. Jasmine had never seen her so drunk before.

'I don't want to talk about him.'

'Did you love him, Jazz?'

'What, no! Don't be ridiculous.'

'You know, what's funny about you, Jazz, is that you don't even know what you've got. I have to work so hard to get a fraction of the attention you do. I think I'm in love with Tim. I can't stop thinking about him.'

'You're drunk,' Jasmine said dismissively.

280

'You don't even know how beautiful you are. Everyone could see that Mr Morrell had a thing for you, it didn't just come out of nowhere. You are so oblivious to the way boys look at you.'

'You're being silly now.'

'You don't see it, but I see it. You're like, magical, or something. I wish I had your life.'

'I have to tell you something' – Jasmine knew it was now or never – 'about me and Tim.'

'When?'

'Last weekend, after you left.'

Felicity shrugged as though it was inevitable. 'Was he using me to try and make you jealous? That's a first.'

'I don't know. I don't think he's like other guys. He's not normal. I can't even begin to guess why he kissed either one of us. I wish I could go back and change what happened. I feel like such an idiot for falling for it.'

'Why would you feel like an idiot? Did you sleep with him?'

'Promise you won't tell anyone.'

'Are you OK? I thought you were waiting for Mr Right.'

'Just do me a favour and stay away from him. I don't trust him.' Jasmine tried to impart how serious she was with her expression, but Felicity could barely focus.

'Don't trust him, or don't trust *me*?'

'You're not listening to me. I think he's dangerous. I don't want you to get hurt.'

'You're paranoid,' Felicity retorted, lying back down.

Jasmine considered telling her about that night at the fair with Mr Morrell, or showing her the photograph, but she didn't know what she would do. Felicity never let things go. She would want to know everything and Jasmine couldn't be sure that she would be entirely discreet about the whole thing. Felicity wasn't quite the detective she thought she was, particularly as she was usually half cut. When she looked across, Felicity had fallen asleep. Jasmine snuggled in and watched the TV; the repetition of the theme tune and gags she had seen a hundred times before were soothing. She didn't realise until she was out of her own house how tense she had been there. The fact that she felt more relaxed here, with the sound of Felicity's heartbroken mother blasting power ballads through the house, just went to show how bad things were at home. The muffled sound of Whitney Houston accompanied by canned laughter served as a lullaby, Jasmine snuggling into Felicity and closing her eyes, just for a moment.

*

When Jasmine woke up she was alone. Felicity's door was open and she could hear shouting coming from the kitchen. She couldn't tell whose voice was whose; the power dynamic in this house was not the norm, as Felicity and her mother were more like resentful siblings than mother and daughter. There was a lot of love there – Jasmine had seen it – but there was a lot of anger, too. On both sides. It was getting dark outside. She tied her hair into a loose bun and picked up her phone.

'Jasmine?' her dad answered.

'Could you come and get me from Felicity's house?'

'It's barely ten, I thought you wanted picking up at midnight.'

'Felicity's asleep already and I'd rather come home,' Jasmine lied.

'Have you been drinking?'

'I haven't, I promise.'

'OK, well, I'm still not home yet. We thought we had a bit longer. I'll call Tim to come and get you. Just keep an eye out. Text me when you're home.'

Before Jasmine had time to object, he was gone.

Lights appeared on the street outside Felicity's house as Tim pulled up in his car.

In the car Jasmine tried to remember how she had behaved the last time Tim drove her anywhere. She was aware that she couldn't let on that she'd seen the photo, that she knew he was up to something. She was too tired to feign lust, praying that she didn't have to.

They drove past the turning they should have taken and instead Tim headed to the eastern side of town and through the ford. It wasn't the way home.

She looked over at Tim; he stared at the road unflinchingly. Where was he taking her? She couldn't jump from a moving car but her heart was bursting out of her chest.

'Where are we going?' she asked, trying to sound a lot calmer than she felt.

'I want to show you something.'

He drove up to the highest point on Cliff Road, stopping next to a path that overlooked Pennington Point, the place where Mr Morrell had committed suicide. The place where she suspected Tim had pushed him from.

Tim opened the door and helped Jasmine out of the car, keeping hold of her wrist as they walked down the path towards the clifftops. She couldn't speak. She couldn't do anything but follow him. It was still so warm and there was no breeze at all; the air was so stagnant that she could barely feel herself breathing. The silence around them magnified the sense of danger. They reached the edge of the path and the sea stretched out before them. It looked magnificent and inviting in a deep dark indigo, a star-peppered sky above them with a full moon painting haphazard stripes of light across the water.

'We had better get back home,' Jasmine said, aware that she wasn't far from the edge, a few metres maybe, and it would be nothing for him to pick her up and toss her over the side. Jasmine could see the narrative now. *Lovesick girl commits suicide in the same spot that teacher lover took his life just days before.* Her parents would probably even believe it.

'We'll go back in a minute. I just wanted to talk to you. To make you understand.' She felt his hand on the small of her back and she resisted every urge that was telling her to turn back and run away. *Stay calm.*

'Let's just go home,' she said. Why had he brought her here?

'Are you cold?' he asked, rubbing her back a little as he got closer. She should never have got in the car with him. She should have walked home, it wasn't even that far.

'No, actually I'm warm. I'm just tired,' she said, pulling away. 'Why did you bring me here?'

'I thought it might help. I know you feel guilty about what happened to your teacher. I thought being here and seeing this might make you feel better.'

'Why would being here make me feel better? And besides nothing "happened" to him, he killed himself. Didn't he?'

'You know what I mean.' He smiled strangely and turned away from her.

'Did you hurt him? After that night, did you come back and hurt him?'

'How would you feel if I did?'

'Afraid . . . of you,' she said honestly.

'There's no reason to be afraid of me, Jasmine. Do you think people like him change? Do you think they deserve another chance? I don't. I don't think they can change. You've got to believe me though, Jasmine, I would never hurt you.'

'I want to go home,' she said. She believed that he hadn't brought her there to hurt her, but had he brought her there to confess? He was different up here; there was none of his usual bravado, no simmering arrogance. There was something a little out of control about him on this grassy clifftop.

He turned and looked at her, studied her even. 'I bet you wished he was dead, didn't you? When they were asking you all those questions about him. Asking you if he touched you? I bet you thought about different ways you could make it all go away, make him disappear.'

'No! of course not. I want to go home now. You're scaring me.'

He moved forwards quickly and grabbed her by the shoulders, staring into her eyes. 'We don't have much time, Jasmine. Things are going to happen, things you won't understand. I just want you to know I'm not the bad guy here. He was a bad person and he deserved what happened to him. People like him don't deserve mercy. They deserve to die.'

'Please take me home,' she begged, tears streaking her cheeks. The strangest look appeared on Tim's face, a new expression that she hadn't seen before, desperate somehow, almost pleading with her to understand. He let go, shaking the unfamiliar expression off and putting on a face she recognised.

'I'm sorry. I never meant for any of this. This isn't what I wanted. I'll take you home.'

She walked ahead to the car, glad to be away from the cliff's edge. Why bring her to this place? If it was sex he wanted from her, then he had had ample opportunity in the past. For the first time he had let his mask slip though. One way or another she was going to find out what he wanted.

She was going to get into the guest house and see what he was hiding.

When the engine turned over she was finally able to take a breath. As they stopped the car at the traffic lights she could see him watching her; she didn't want to face him right now but she could feel him imploring her to. The road was empty, the light was green, but he didn't move. She turned towards him. He could have pushed her off the cliff, no one would have seen it. Instead he looked her in the eyes, tears hovering at the edges of his, the truest face he had shown her yet. He seemed so sad, so completely bereft. She didn't believe that you could fake that.

Chapter Thirty-Nine

Now

I never make it to the woods, instead I seek out a pub and console myself in there. My mother worked here over Christmas once, I remember; they asked her to fill in for a sick member of staff as she was a regular. She would tell stories of how much fun it was, but I think she thought it was beneath her. I think she thought lots of things were. Being in here makes me feel closer to her, or at least a version of her.

The television on the wall is playing the news. There's lots of speculation on why Hannah and the soldier were buried in the woods together – were they having an affair that went wrong?

Hannah's father was being interrogated, as the woods are near his house. But the woods are near lots of houses – this town isn't that big – so technically the woods are near every house here. It wouldn't take many people longer than ten minutes to get there by car. One of the stories circulating is that he found out this man was sleeping with his daughter and killed them both in a fit of rage. That sounds quite far-fetched to me, but the media are running with it. I find a newspaper on the counter with a picture of Hannah on the front. Mandy Green has already been relegated to page seven. As she moves further back in the newspaper more and more people will forget about her, save her mother, who will never be able to move on.

My phone is ringing. I look at the display and see it's Chris. I haven't called him in days, resigned to the fact that he has finally come to his senses and decided to get rid of me. This place has a way of making me forget time. Is it wrong that I hadn't thought about the children for several hours, maybe even longer?

'Chris?'

'Hi,' he says softly.

'I didn't think you were speaking to me?'

'I wasn't. I'm sorry.'

'How are you, how are the kids?'

'We're good. Do you still want us to come down? We can if you want us to.'

'It's a long way. You don't have to. I'm almost done here now anyway.'

'I saw on the news that they found an old body buried in the woods. Was it the girl you knew?'

'Yes.'

'I'm sorry, love.'

I start to cry and I'm not sure why; it's not like I was good friends with her. 'It's good for her family to have closure now,' I say, even though her father is a suspect, even though I know more than he does. I could tell the police things that would shift their focus entirely.

'We'll head down in the morning, OK?'

'It would be good to see you. I love you,' I say and hang up before he has a chance to not say it back.

A clock has been started. I need to find out the truth about Mandy's disappearance before my family come, before her body turns up. I need to purge the old me again and become the wife and mother I was before; she wasn't perfect, but she would be a good place to start. I just need one more drink first.

It's getting darker when I go outside. I have lost count of the number of drinks I have had, and I stumble forwards in in the half light and grab for a tree planted in the pavement to stop me from falling. More memories surface of my life before I left, but I push them down. It all goes back to that one summer. Being here has made me realise all the other people I miss. Like my mother. How can I move forward without confronting the devils of my past?

As I walk unsteadily forwards I hear an engine rev nearby. I look around but I can't see anything. I know it's there, though, I can hear the gentle hum of the engine like the breath of a stalker. The car headlights in the street are all dark and my vision is blurred, my temples throbbing. I don't know why I can't control myself here, it's never just one glass. I don't do this at home.

I keep walking, my destination programmed into me. I feel my knee stinging so I know I have fallen at some point. I perch on the edge of a garden wall, the ever present sound of a car engine nearby. I wonder if it's just in my head, swirling around with the rest of my cacophony of thoughts. When I start to walk again, muscle memory takes me in the direction I need to go. I walked this hill many times in the past, sometimes alone, some-times with friends, sometimes sober, sometimes drunk.

I hear the engine again, closer this time.

I shake my head to try and get the sound out but it stays. I look to the road behind me but there's nothing there. As I turn back a full beam of light shines straight in my eyes, and I hear a voice, a voice I thought I had forgotten, a voice I am not sure is even really there. In my mind I have replayed this voice often, trying to cling onto any kindness. It's different in my memory, softer somehow. Now it sounds jarring and desperate.

'You shouldn't have come. It's not safe for you here,' it says, so familiar.

The light is so bright I can't see anything but white. I look up to the sky and fractals of light remnants bounce around my head, the dizziness taking over. I stumble backwards and start to run. I don't stop until I can no longer hear cars or see the road. Moments later I am behind the street on a bench under a willow tree, I don't know how long I was running, all I know is that I am fast. Even under the influence, I can move faster than my pursuer and I know the car can't get into this park. I lie back on the bench, my vision returning to normal. If I can just close my eyes for a second, I can regain my strength and try again. The moment of clarity comes and I stand. I'm stronger than this. I am getting closer, I can feel it. The only thing left is to find out the truth I was so afraid of knowing all those years ago. I need to find the driver of that car. I need find out what happened to Mandy.

Chapter Forty

Then

Watching from the window, Jasmine waited for Tim to leave. The more she thought about his erratic and inexplicable behaviour on the clifftop the more she knew she had to get into his rooms. She waited what seemed like an eternity before she heard the guest house door open. She saw him checking that no one was around before leaving with his backpack slung over his shoulder. She pulled back from the window a little as he glanced upwards. Her room was dark, and she was sure he couldn't see her, but if he could then he showed no sign of it. He left by the back gate and she jumped out of bed.

Downstairs Jasmine went straight for the key, then peered outside to check that Tim's car was gone. It was that time of day when everyone was either still in bed or had just left to complete errands and a bizarre silence descended on the neighbourhood. She couldn't even hear the neighbour's kids with their relentless trampolining. It was now or never.

As Jasmine pushed the key in the lock, nausea crept over her, as though she were crossing a line that couldn't be uncrossed. Every part of her knew he wouldn't be amenable if he found her inside his house; the way he had reacted when he caught her at the threshold before had shown how he felt about her being inside there. Still, she pushed forward. There was no more time; she had to get to the truth.

Moving slowly and carefully through the property, Jasmine noticed how untouched everything was. The first room she came across was a small lounge with the sofa from their last house in it, and a wave of nostalgia hit her. But there was no television – in fact, aside from the items her parents had decorated the room with, there was no furniture at all.

Jasmine walked through to the bathroom. A bar of soap, toothbrush and toothpaste sat on the sink. In the cupboard was a tin of something called pomade; she didn't know what that was.

In the double bedroom there was just enough room for a metal-framed IKEA double bed, and the back wall was fitted with slatted louvre doors to hide the clothes rail and shelving. There was nothing in Tim's bedroom. The bed was bare, with no sheets. Instead, there was a sleeping bag in its sleeve on the chair and a pair of binoculars on the sill. Had he ever even lain on the bed before or did he just sit in that chair, watching the house from the window? All those accidental meetings in the garden were no accident at all.

It would have taken Tim less than five minutes to clear this house of all his belongings, if you could even call a sleeping bag and some personal hygiene products that. Jasmine walked past Tim's bed, which looked brand new and untouched with the plastic wrapper still on the mattress. Her uneasiness grew, the mystery around him increasing. The first wardrobe was empty, as were the second and third. Where were his things? There were two more doors left. Her palms got sweatier as she reached for the handles. She opened the doors and saw a T-shirt and jeans on the shelf. Just one spare outfit? Did he keep things in his car still? Maybe that was it. Her father had told her that Tim had lived out of his car – maybe he just couldn't make the transition. She paused before she opened the final door, terrified of what she might find in there.

A weapon? A body? He could be hiding anything. She closed her eyes as she pulled the handle and then opened them again to see it was an empty shelving unit at a first glance, but when she bent right down, she could see the messenger bag he had tried to hide from her before, pushed deep into the corner. She reached down and pulled it out. She could already tell from the weight of it that it was full of papers. She let out a breath, relieved it didn't contain a severed head or anything equally distressing.

Perched on the edge of the bed, Jasmine lay the bag down next to her. Carefully pressing the sides of the plastic clip that locked the bag she released the flap and reached inside, a part of her anticipating that something might bite her. She ran her fingers along the surface of the contents as if somehow she could discern what they were without actually having to look at them, as if this was somehow less of an intrusion, as if that in itself was forgivable. Her fingers dragged on the paper and she knew it was a photograph. Aware that time was no longer on her side, she pulled the photographs out of the bag.

The first photo was of a place. It was familiar to Jasmine, but she didn't know why. It showed the front of a building, painted green and run down, with cracks all over the front. She had seen it before but she had no idea when, or where, or why. The next photo was more familiar.

It was her parents' bedroom.

A chill ran through her as she saw her mother's clothes laid out on the bed side by side. There were four more photographs like that one, including photos of all of Lisa's underwear. Tim must have taken some of those photographs when he was in the house alone; others were taken at night. Jasmine tensed; she knew exactly which night. She couldn't think about that right now; she had to focus on what she was there for. These photos of her parents' room were like an inventory of some sort. Why would he want this?

The next photograph stopped her in her tracks. It was Jasmine's bedroom, her clothes, every single one of them, laid out and photographed, just like her mother's had been. Whatever his perversion was, it made less and less sense to her by the second. She died a little when she saw he had been through her laundry and photographed it as well, including her dirty underwear. Next were more photos of inside the house, including all of her and her mother's jewellery, with some items circled, although she had no idea why. She felt dizzy with fear. Everything was so methodical, so clinical. It was like a dossier of every part of her family's life. The reality of the danger she was in was starting to hit home – these photos were not normal, they weren't even normal perversion. It would almost make more sense if he had photos of them all sleeping or getting undressed. This though? This was like a mission.

The next photos were of a different quality, much older, well-worn at the edges. The first was of the green house again, a similar picture to the one before but a much older copy. She turned the page to uncover the next photograph, catching her breath instinctively.

The first thing she saw was red. The tones varied from bright, luminous streaks across the top half of the photograph and deep chocolatey red pooling at the bottom of the picture. Blood. So much blood. The picture showed the corpse of a young woman, in her late teens at most, barely recognisable as human. She was swathed in blood, with not a patch of her skin untouched by the red cloak of death. Who was she? Why did he have this photograph? Her mouth ran dry; she didn't want to turn to the next picture but her fingers had started moving independently. She could tell these photos were real. They weren't pretty or stylised enough to be anything else. She felt sick to the stomach.

She knew, she knew from the moment Tim came into their lives he was trouble. She should have made more of a fuss; she should have made her parents kick him out then. Every decision she had made since meeting him had been wrong. He had played her exactly right. Making her doubt what she knew inside to be true. She should have told her parents about that night when they went away. She should have told her parents about the photo she found.

The next image was of the same girl, but a close-up picture of her face. If the photo were in black and white Jasmine might have assumed she was sleeping; she looked so peaceful. But it wasn't, and everything was red. She was a pretty girl; Jasmine could see that much. Her hair looked black, but that could have just been a trick of the light.

The next picture confused her. The girl was positioned differently. It took a few moments to fully comprehend that it was another girl entirely. She looked through the photographs with more speed now, uncovering girl after girl lying in pools of their own blood. The pictures seemed to be taken with different cameras, which made her think they'd been taken over a period of time. Jasmine's heart was pounding, and she could barely breathe.

She heard the distant click of the latch on the back gate followed by the screech of its hinges. He was back. If he found her there, there would be no conversations. She would be one of these photographs – one of these girls. She had to hurry.

She gathered the photographs quickly and stuffed them back into the bag. Why was he back so soon? She put the bag back where she had found it and then looked around for a place to hide. It was either the wardrobe or under the bed. In a split decision she opted for the wardrobe; it felt less exposed and she would feel more vulnerable lying down. She opened one of the doors and slid inside the empty compartment as fast as she could. She clamped her hand over her mouth as tears streamed down her face, closing her eyes tight as the door to the guest house opened and Tim walked inside.

Chapter Forty-One

Jasmine's fingers trembled. She had never been so afraid. She tried not to breathe loudly, to give herself away. She should have just told her parents about her suspicions. Now no one knew where she was.

Tim walked into the bedroom and threw his backpack on the floor. She could just about see his legs through the slatted louvre doors as he walked. She had seen what he was capable of, what he had done to all those women and maybe what he planned to do to her. As he was leaving the bedroom she let out the breath she had been holding in. He stopped and turned around, looking around the room. Suddenly, he stormed forwards, straight for the wardrobe. But it was the one next to Jasmine. Her relief was profound. Had she put the bag back exactly as she had found it? She couldn't be sure. Her heart was in her mouth as he pulled out the messenger bag, heaved it onto the bed, then opened it.

'Come out.'

The fear crystallised inside Jasmine, acute, intense and inescapable. She was going to die.

A second later the door to the wardrobe opened and Tim grabbed Jasmine by the arm and pulled her out into the room.

'Please, don't hurt me,' she sobbed, her legs buckling underneath her as the fear took hold. It would be hours before anyone was home, hours before anyone found her body. She imagined her hair tangled and slick with blood. She imagined her parents finding her, or maybe he would kill them too, throw them all in the hole he had dug for her father's resistance pool and then disappear.

'I told you not to come in here!' Tim roared, his eyes wild with fury.

'I'm sorry. I'm so sorry,' Jasmine said, shrinking and cowering beneath his towering form.

'Did you find what you were looking for? Are you happy now?' He gestured at the bed. Did he want her to lie down? Maybe this was what he had wanted all along, for her to be afraid.

'Please. Just let me go. I didn't see anything.'

He grabbed her chin and directed her face towards the bed. The bag was open, and the pictures were spread across it. Red.

'Have a good look.'

'I won't tell anyone. I'll just forget I ever saw that, and you can go.'

'I'm not going anywhere. I'm not done here.'

Jasmine started to sob; she couldn't control the tears as they came. She had never wanted her parents more than she did right now. She felt so small, so young and so helpless. She knew his strength, she had felt his muscles pressed against her. Jasmine tried to pull her wrist free, but he just locked his hand even tighter around it; it was barely an effort for him.

'Please . . .' she begged, scarcely hearing her own muffled voice through the sobs.

'Just sit down and let me explain. I didn't want it to be like this.'

He pushed her onto the bed but yanked her forward as she went to lie back. He looked annoyed at her assumption that he would assault her that way. As if it would be unthinkable.

'I saw what you did to those girls,' Jasmine whimpered, terrified she was going to set him off again.

'It's not what you think.'

'Those girls aren't really dead?'

'Oh, they are dead. I didn't kill them though.'

Jasmine hadn't expected him to say that; then again she wasn't sure what she'd expected when she walked into this room. It wasn't anything like this. Was he insane, had he killed these women and forgotten?

He reached into the messenger bag and pulled out a crumpled tissue. He unwrapped it to reveal a necklace. Jasmine's necklace. Was this his trophy? The thing he would rub between his fingers in order to remember the excitement of the moment she died at his hands? She had read enough about serial killers to know that they liked to keep a memento of their kills.

Tim grabbed two photographs from the bed and handed them to her. One was a folded picture of a girl with a bright smile, billowing black hair and the most mesmerising dark brown eyes. The other picture was of a dead body.

'What is this? Why did you steal my necklace? What are you going to do to me? Are you going to kill me?' she said, desperately trying to hold back her tears.

'That necklace belonged to this girl. Her name is Rosa. She's wearing it in the picture, see?'

Jasmine examined the picture and saw that she was wearing a necklace like hers.

'There's probably loads of those necklaces

around. It could have come from anywhere. Where did you get this picture?'

He unfolded the picture and Jasmine saw that Tim was standing with Rosa.

'This was taken before my fiancée went missing. When they found her, she had been murdered. Look at the necklace in the picture; it's the same one. You think when they make each one, they put all those tiny little glass beads in exactly the same order?'

The necklace Rosa was wearing was identical to Jasmine's necklace. How was that possible? Jasmine was struggling with what he was telling her, what he seemed so desperate for her to comprehend.

'I don't understand . . . what are you saying?'

'The last person to see Rosa alive was your father. I think he killed her. I think he killed all these girls.'

Chapter Forty-Two

Jasmine stared at Tim, the stranger who lived in their house. Had he completely lost his mind? She kept looking back at the picture of the girl. Something about the girl's face stirred some recognition in her, but she couldn't quite place it. Was this Tim's manipulating his way out of trouble after she had found his sick and twisted secret? That didn't explain the necklace though.

'Tell me who you really are. Don't lie to me this time. No more lies.' She could hear her voice shaking as she spoke.

'OK. I promise.'

Jasmine folded her arms, partly for security but also so that he would see that she meant business. He had to know she was no longer vulnerable to his charm. She just wanted to know the truth. At least she thought she did.

'Is Tim even your real name?'

'It is. My name is Tim Fulton. I am a soldier in the British army, currently on medical leave. I came here looking for the person who killed my fiancée. Every lead, every avenue led me to your father.'

'You're lying,' she spat.

'We can ask him, if you want? Show him those photos and see what he does.'

She couldn't tell if she believed him or not; she had believed him before and he had been lying.

Except he seemed so convinced of what he was saying.

'Is that why you're here? What were you planning on doing to him?'

'I want him to admit it. She didn't deserve what he did to her.'

Jasmine shook her head. She couldn't accept what he was saying.

'My dad didn't do it. There's no way. He's lovely, ask anyone. He's not capable of those hideous things. Whoever did that to those girls was a monster and my father is the furthest thing from a monster on this planet.'

'Are you telling me there's nothing you find strange about him? Even just these past few weeks here I can see that he's off. There's something missing.'

'No. You're seeing what you want to see. He's not what you're saying.'

Tim ignored her. 'I wasn't sure at first, but now I know he did it. I know he killed Rosa.'

Jasmine knew she had to keep him talking 'til she could get away from him and warn her father. 'Tell me about her, where is this supposed to have happened?' Her head was spinning. Everything he was saying was a lie, but she could tell he was utterly convinced of it. He must be insane, there was no other explanation for it. He was mistaken.

'I was stationed in Belize,' he began. That explained why he'd been in the photo of her parents, at least. Maybe Rosa gave her necklace to Lisa and Frank, and that was why Jasmine had it? 'We were taking part in three months of covert jungle training at the Batsub base. While we were there, I met a girl from the village near the training ground. She was incredible, warm, loving and we fell in love. She was the world to me.'

'When was this?'

'Back in 1998.'

Jasmine felt her mouth go dry; that was when they had gone to Belize for the summer.

'So, what do you think happened?' she challenged.

'She worked in the foodbank in Ladyville. I met

311

her when we were delivering some stuff from the base there; that was one of my duties. We worked with the locals and wanted to help out. It was almost instant between us. That spark. She had grown up in an orphanage and was really dedicated to giving to people who were less fortunate than her,' he said, a smile on his face she hadn't seen before, a memory of something cherished but lost. He was obviously very broken; maybe he didn't even know how broken he was. He had convinced himself of something that just couldn't be true.

Jasmine stood up. She needed to move around, her pulse racing as she tried to understand what he was saying. He must be out of his mind. But the timing was right and she thought she could remember the food bank. She felt sick as she realised that she had been contemplating what Tim was suggesting, just for a moment.

'I remember the foodbank,' she admitted. 'The charity we went there with got our group to build new shelving in the storage room and we painted it all the colours of the rainbow.'

It was as if Tim hadn't heard her.

'One day, near the end of the summer, she went out and never came back. The last time her colleagues spoke to her, she was on her way to the bus stop to go into the city. The police searched for her, but they just thought she had run away. Lots of young women disappear in the city for a myriad reasons. Finding her just wasn't a priority. But I spoke to as many people as I could, and the last time she was seen, she was talking with an English man who matched the description of your father.'

Jasmine could hear the words he was saying, but she could hardly bear to listen. It was just a misunderstanding. He might think he knew what had happened to his fiancée, but he was wrong. She guessed he might be lying to himself to avoid facing the fact Rosa hadn't felt the same way about him as he did about her. She'd probably just left.

'How do you know she didn't just run away?'

'Because they found her body,' he told her, a flash of anger crossing his face. 'Just before I left, they pulled parts of her out of the river. She had been dumped in there and the alligators got to her.'

'That must have been awful,' she said, 'but that doesn't mean it was my father. There were forty people working in our group; it could have been one of the other men. And if she was in pieces like you say, then how do you have that picture then? Is that her? The woman covered in blood?' She asked. She didn't even know if anything he was saying was real. Was this another diversion tactic of his? Was he still trying to confuse her? She had found his pictures, so he might tell any lie to stop her from calling the police until he got what he wanted. If only she could figure out what that was.

'That's her. None of the other men matched the description that was given to me. There is no doubt in my mind that your father killed her.'

'So where did that photograph come from if they didn't find her body until later?' Jasmine insisted.

'I got this photograph from a box I found in your parents' bedroom.'

His words had the desired impact. Jasmine felt as though a jolt of electricity had shot through her.

'You're lying.'

'I swear, I'm not.'

'This doesn't make any sense! Who are those other girls then? Why are there so many?'

'Those dead girls are all photos I found in that box. I don't know who the others are yet. Maybe you can help me find out.'

'I'm not helping you! You must be crazy if you think I'm going to listen to any of this.' She went to walk past him, but Tim thrust the necklace into her hand.

'Where did you get this?' he asked.

'It was a gift for my birthday. My eleventh birthday.'

'When you were in Belize?'

'That doesn't mean anything. You're trying to trick me.'

'How could I know that it was from that year you stayed in Belize? It could have been any birthday, but you got it around the time my Rosa disappeared. I know because I bought it for her in the market in Ladyville.'

'Why did you come here?' Jasmine said, starting to cry again. 'Why are you trying to hurt us? Did you sleep with me just so you could go through my things? Just so you could try and trick me into believing all of this nonsense?'

'I'm not proud of what happened. I couldn't have you being suspicious of me. I could tell that you knew straight away I was lying. I hadn't factored in that you would be older and smarter. I just needed to distract you enough until I got proof.'

'It's easy to fake a photo if you know what you're doing. How do I know this isn't all part of some bizarre scam or something? You haven't exactly been honest with me from the get-go. If this photo is what you say it is, and my father supposedly killed your fiancée, then why didn't you go to the police once you had the proof? Why did you stay here?'

'I watched your family as much as I could from the outside. Once I knew I was on the right track with your parents I became friends with them and made them trust me.'

'So everything about you is a lie? You're not this wonderful man who goes round helping people in need, it's all part of the act to get to my father?'

'I'm not a bad person, he is,' he snapped, rubbing at his temples as though he were trying to clear his thoughts, get them in order. He seemed confused now, less convinced of the truth he was trying to sell her.

She could tell he hadn't anticipated this much resistance from her. He was desperate for her to believe him, without question. He was becoming unhinged. She needed to get out of that room, and soon.

'I don't want to hear this. You have to start being honest with me. You have to tell me if you killed Mr Morrell. Did you go back and hurt him?' She spoke softly; she wanted him to think of her as an ally, as someone he could trust. She had to get out of there; if he thought she was going to run and tell the police then he would never let her go.

'I swear, I didn't. I wouldn't.'

'So, he really did kill himself?'

'Maybe, or maybe your father helped him. I do believe he loves you, Jasmine, as much as he is capable of loving anything,' he said. He seemed to be calming down. The less she resisted him the more chance she had of getting out of there alive.

'So what do we do now?' she asked, not only wondering about the immediate situation but about what he might have planned next.

'I want you to help me.'

'Help you do what?'

'Find out who all these girls are. The photos were all jumbled together in the box and so there are no dates to go by. There's no information whatsoever, in fact. Just girl after girl, butchered as if she meant nothing. Your father did that.'

'I feel sick,' Jasmine said, sitting back down, unsure how to carry on from there. The more she pretended that what he was saying was even remotely reasonable, the more seeds of doubt infiltrated her thoughts. He couldn't be telling the truth. Could he? It all came back to that necklace. She knew her father had given it to her; the only question now was where he got it from. At some point before it belonged to Jasmine, it had belonged to Rosa. Was her father the only person who could have taken it from one and given it to the other?

'All of these girls have families. Every single one

of them deserves better than this.' He thrust the photo of his fiancée in her face again. She didn't want to look.

'I'm not going to help you. Go now and I won't tell anyone. If you're not a bad person like you say, then you need to leave us alone,' Jasmine implored, afraid to entertain his theory for a moment longer, afraid that she was starting to believe him.

'Look at those pictures. Don't they deserve justice?'

'What you're suggesting can't be true. It just can't.'

'Just give me today at least. Please. I've been trying to identify these other women but I don't even know where to start. Together we might have more luck.'

Why was he willing to let her go? If he had been the one who hurt those girls would he have wasted this time trying to convince her of anything? Surely it would have been quicker just to dispatch her.

'I will give you an hour to get out. After that I'm calling the police.'

'If you call the police, your dad will go to prison. Is that what you want? Prove me wrong if you can, just tell me where to look, tell me what to look for.'

'Don't you want him to go to prison?' she asked.

'I do but I need more evidence to make sure. Please just give me time to find some more.'

Jasmine thought about his proposition for a moment. She didn't know why she was even considering doing what Tim wanted, but there was something in the back of her mind telling her she must get to the truth. She couldn't live with the niggling doubt in her mind that Tim had put there. She believed that *he* believed what he was saying to her, but she wanted to prove him wrong.

'I need some air,' Jasmine said, her nausea getting stronger. She couldn't look at those photos for another second.

He didn't stop her as she walked calmly from the room, out into the small corridor and then into the garden. She gulped but couldn't get the warm air into her fast enough. She thought about those women, their photographs in a box under the bed. She knew the box Tim was talking about. She had never looked in there because it was her father's box. She wondered if this was why her father was so adamant about respecting each other's privacy; he wanted to keep *his* secrets private. Jasmine thought back to the way he'd expertly dismantled the fish when they went to Wales together on family trips and she was reminded of the cuts on the women's bodies. Her father handled a knife like an expert, like someone with a lot of practice.

The sun beat down on her, and she felt dizzy as the images of those poor girls' faces appeared in her mind like a highlight reel. She could feel herself falling but had no power to stop it. The last thought in her mind before she lost consciousness was that her father was a stranger.

Chapter Forty-Three

Now

The end of the road, that's where I am. Both figuratively and literally. Still dressed in yesterday's clothes, awoken this morning by an eager spaniel who was sniffing and licking my hand as I lay on the bench where I had intended to stop for only a few moments but instead slept the whole night.

I walk down the road I once lived on. The good memories of this house completely overshadowed by the bad. I can't see it yet, but I can feel it, like the sinister black mansion in a horror movie, looming with malicious intent. I hope it will be a hole in the ground when I finally reach it, even though, in my mind's eye, it's still the same as the day I left. I approach a bend in the road I have walked down a hundred times before, knowing full well what I will see when I take those next few steps. The sight that was once so welcome instils fear in me now. It's just a house. It's just a house. It's just a house.

Chapter Forty-Four

Then

Jasmine banged her fist against the door of Felicity's house. She could hear Carol's music blaring again. She pounded harder and pushed the doorbell several times. The door swung open to reveal Carol in her dressing gown. She always had a smile for Jasmine.

'Felicity!' she screamed up the stairs as she made her way back into the kitchen and closed the door. The house vibrated as the music started again.

Jasmine sat on the sofa in Felicity's lounge. She could tell by the look on Felicity's face that she looked ghostly. She had rushed out of the house as soon as she could and turned up at Felicity's, banging frantically on the door for someone to let her in.

'You need sugar,' Felicity's mother said as she appeared with a glass of pineapple juice. It was the most motherly thing Jasmine had ever seen Carol do.

'What happened?' Felicity asked.

'I just don't feel well. I'll be fine. I think I've got a summer cold coming,' Jasmine said, desperate to get rid of Carol so she could confide in Felicity.

She thought about the wisdom of leaving Tim at her house. How would she explain any of this to her parents? She guessed it wasn't her place to explain anything to anyone. Maybe Tim would be gone by the time she went back and she could forget all of this. Pretend that she had never seen those photos and pretend that the necklace she cherished wasn't ripped from the neck of a dead girl. The thought of wearing that necklace ever again made her want to cry.

'Come on, tell me what's going on. Is it Tim? Did something happen?' Felicity asked as her mother left the room.

Jasmine nodded and started to cry.

'It's not what you think. I don't even know what it is. I'm so confused.'

'You look like you've seen a ghost. Tell me what's going on. I won't say anything, I promise.

Did he hurt you or something? Oh my God, did he force himself on you?'

'What? No, it's nothing like that.' Jasmine took a deep breath. 'I broke into the guest house when he was out, to try and find out more about him. He's been behaving really weirdly. I was going to tell you, but I wanted to find out what the deal was first.'

'Oh my God! What did you find out?' Felicity said, clearly trying not to look too excited. She lived for drama.

'I found some photos, horrible ones, dead girls and stuff.'

'What, like snuff movie type stuff?'

'Like . . . serial killer type stuff.'

'What?' Felicity's mouth fell open. 'Whose photos were they?'

'He said they were my dad's. He said my dad killed his girlfriend.' Jasmine could feel her breath shortening as she spoke. Was this really happening? Those photographs though, *someone* did that to those women and Jasmine was faced with two possibilities. One, that Tim killed them and was covering his tracks because she had found him out. Could she really let him go without calling the police if she truly believed that to be the case? The main issue with this theory was that he could have killed her too, at any time. Two, that Tim was telling the truth and her father, Frank, had murdered those women. Should she confront her father? Would he even admit it to her if it was true? And what if he did? What if it was true? Should she beg him to stop? She didn't know what to do. She looked at Felicity, whose mouth was still open.

'That's mad. Are you being serious? What are you talking about? Is Tim off his head or what?'

'I don't know what to do. I should be scared of him, I *am* scared of him. But I don't know, I can't help thinking about it. What if he isn't lying?'

'You've got to tell your parents.'

'What if he's right?'

'That's insane,' Felicity scoffed. 'He's not right. He's some kind of con artist or something. Who are all the girls your dad is supposed to have killed?'

'You know how every year we go away to help somewhere? According to Tim it was all a lie. My father was just trying to get access to young women no one would look for. The countries we went to were already overloaded with violence, so who would miss a girl or two? We heard stories like that all the time. If you picked the right girl they just didn't seem to look for them. If some other girl with no family was targeted instead of Rosa, then Tim wouldn't even have been looking, no one would.'

'If he's even telling the truth . . .' Felicity shook her head. 'Your dad wouldn't do anything like that. No way. You have to call the police and get Tim out of your house.'

'I don't want to call the police and I don't want to tell my parents. What if the police believe Tim? He is such a good liar.'

'What are you going to do then?'

'I don't know. What would you do?'

'We should tell my mum. She knows how to deal with scumbags.'

'You don't even like your mum.'

'Dan's gone now so she's pretty straight at the moment. Honestly, she has dealt with more than her fair share of liars and manipulators; she always comes out the other side. He's probably just a chancer. Trust me, she'll know what to do.'

Tim was wrong about her father. He had to be. Jasmine couldn't ignore the fact that she'd found those images in Tim's room, not her parents'. And Tim was a proven liar, over and over . . . yet in the back of her mind his accusations turned over again and again, gaining more credibility with every passing moment.

She remembered getting the necklace from her father on her eleventh birthday. It was nothing but glass seed beads interspersed with sequins, hand-made. All tiny and imperfect and not expensive in any way, but she had always loved it, loved the way the light caught the beads. Jasmine now wondered if he'd taken it before he killed Rosa. Those creeping thoughts were impossible to reconcile with her own understanding of who her father was, though. He looked after people; he bent over backwards to make sure the people around him were happy. Was it guilt that drove him to be so generous and charitable, or was it all part of his mask? Did he do those things so suspicion would never fall on him? She couldn't figure this out on her own; she would have to tell Felicity's mother.

Chapter Forty-Five

Now

The front garden is overgrown and looks like it hasn't been touched in years. Dead brown vines cling to the garden wall and the shrubs are a tangled mess, not how I remember things from my childhood. I wonder how the neighbours feel about the state of it. Every other house on this street looks like a contender for some kind of garden competition, with roses and dahlias in every imaginable colour all tastefully arranged and almost certainly trimmed on a daily basis.

I stare at the house. It looks smaller than I remember. It looks derelict; the wood on the front door is blown from water damage and big strips of the black paint have peeled off. I see the brass letterbox is broken, rusted open and twisted. The curtains are pulled across, the lining faded at the folds.

I'm not sure how long I have been standing here. I see the drive is the only thing that looks used, and the space in front of the garage door is clear. Someone has been here recently.

There is no sign of movement at all in the house, so I wonder if I can sneak around the back and through the garden. I had done it before as a teenager, more than once. I take my first step forwards, my guts wrenching and everything in me telling me to just get away from here. I promised myself I would never come back here; I didn't think I ever could. The last night I was here was the night my best friend in the world died.

I walk down the side of the house, past the wheelie bins, and try the back gate. Past the gate the garden is overgrown and looks derelict, a pit in one corner full of old furniture, clothes, bits of wood and metal, ready for some kind of bonfire that never happened. The place is a mess.

Chapter Forty-Six

Then

Jasmine hadn't bitten her nails in years, not since her mother put that awful tasting clear nail polish on in a bid to get her to stop. But now she was chewing on the skin around her thumb nervously as she told Carol what Tim had told her. Felicity's mother stared in silence as Jasmine recounted what she had seen and what Tim had said. Felicity gripped her other hand for support. The silence continued long after Jasmine had finished speaking, until Felicity finally spoke up.

'Well, Mum? What should Jazz do?'

'She needs to tell her parents. I'll come with you if you're afraid. Or we can call them and tell them here, if you'd prefer. Just in case that man is around the house and listening. You can't let him ruin your life, Jazz. There's men out there who just want what's in your wallet or between your legs. Sounds like he's one or the other,' Carol said, lighting a cigarette and taking a long draw from it.

'You don't think he could be telling the truth then?' Jasmine asked, ignoring Carol's crude assessment of Tim, feeling almost like she should defend him.

'He sounds like a complete fantasist, sweetie. You said he was a homeless man before he moved in with your family. Maybe he has mental health issues.'

'Mum!' Felicity shouted with indignation.

'I mean, you hear about stuff like that all the time, don't you? I'll call your house and get your parents to come pick you up. We can tell them together when they get here.'

'Thank you,' Jasmine said as Felicity pulled her out of the room, leaving her mother alone to ring Jasmine's parents. Jasmine couldn't help but feel as if she were blowing everything out of proportion. But she couldn't explain the photos. Where did they come from? Her head was spinning. Nothing made sense anymore. Felicity was the only person she felt she could trust at the moment.

They both sat on the sofa waiting for her parents to arrive, Jasmine's hands firmly clutching Felicity's. They were going to be angry with her for keeping secrets. As much as her father respected privacy, he hated secrets and she had promised him that there would never be anything she couldn't tell him. Even the thought of her parents finding out she had kissed Tim filled her with dread, let alone the other things they would discover.

'What if they throw me out?'

'Don't be silly. Why would they do that?'

'I don't know. I've just got a really bad feeling, Flick.'

'Whatever happens, I've got you. OK? I love you, Jazz, and if they kick you out then you'll come and live here with me,' Felicity said before putting her arms around Jasmine.

The sound of crunching gravel outside alerted them to the arrival of a car, and moments later her father was sitting on the leather recliner opposite Jasmine, Felicity's mother next to her, holding her hand.

'What's this all about?'

Jasmine couldn't find her voice, didn't know how to tell her father what she had found out and how she had even become suspicious in the first place. In the back of her mind she couldn't help wondering if she could trust him, if she even knew him at all. He smiled his funny little half smile, the one he used when he knew she was anxious about something, the one that always calmed her down. How could she have ever doubted him? How could she have listened to a man she barely knew? She had to tell him the truth now, no matter what the consequences were. She remembered all of the secret interactions she had had with Tim and she kicked herself. Once her parents started questioning her then they would find all of it out and they would never trust her again.

Felicity's mother squeezed Jasmine's fingers before speaking.

'Your lodger has been telling Jasmine all kinds of crazy stories and she's a bit spooked, I'm afraid. She found some rather graphic photos in his room and . . .'

'Why were you in his room?'

'Does it matter? He had some really awful pictures, Dad. Dead girls, cut up, blood everywhere.'

'In his room?'

'I asked him what they were, and he told me he thought you killed his girlfriend, Rosa,' Jasmine said.

Her father let out an involuntary bark, like the beginnings of a laugh.

'What on earth would make him think that?'

'He said someone saw her getting into your car. Said you were the last person to see Rosa alive. I think he wants some kind of revenge. I think he wants to hurt you and Mum.'

Her dad shook his head in disbelief, as if he were trying to wrap his head around what she was telling him. He opened his mouth to speak again at least twice but then stopped.

'I'll get us a cup of tea,' Carol said softly before leaving the room. As if tea could in any way repair what was being broken here.

'I think he did something to Mr Morrell, too. I don't think he killed himself.'

'Why do you think that?'

'He just said some weird stuff about it, that's all. The night of the fair, when I bumped into Mr Morrell by the toilets, he grabbed me and Tim came and helped me. He threatened Mr Morrell and not long after he died. Tim's not a good guy; I knew then that he wasn't. The other night he took me up to Pennington Point and was acting really erratically. Saying things about punishment and mercy and other things that didn't make sense.'

'Why didn't you tell us? Oh my God. Did he hurt you? Did he touch you?' Frank said. His voice was full of concern but his eyes were flat. Maybe she was imagining it.

335

'I thought he was just looking out for me in the beginning, but he just got weirder and weirder.'

Jasmine didn't know whether just to come clean about everything, including the conversation she'd had with Tim on the clifftop. She didn't want Frank to know about her secret relationship with this stranger in the house; he would never forgive her; he might never forgive himself. She couldn't remember all the lies Tim had told her over the last few weeks; she could barely even sequence everything that had happened today. All she knew was that she wanted things to go back to how they were before she ever even knew Tim existed. He had done this, he had ruined their lives. Nothing would ever be the same again and she felt she was the one who let it happen. If only she had told her parents about the night he gave them weed and made out with Felicity. They would have got rid of him then. Or maybe she could have told them about the time she spent alone with him. It was no use thinking about that stuff now; it was too late. The damage was done.

'I'm sorry, Dad. Can we just go home?' Jasmine asked just seconds before everything came to the surface and she burst out crying. Her dad came and sat next to her on the sofa, putting his arms around her. She buried her face into his chest and sobbed. How had she messed everything up so badly?

'I'm so sorry, sweetheart. I never should have invited him into our house. I thought he was a good guy, you know? I wish you had said something sooner, I would have got rid of him. And now he's upset you with all these lies about Belize. I'll call the police and then call your mother and warn her not to go home yet. We don't have to go home until he's out of the picture.'

Her dad stood up and left the room. Jasmine could hear him talking on the phone in the hall. Felicity came back into the room and put her arms around Jasmine.

They leaned back into the sofa, still hugging. So many questions were still unanswered but Jasmine didn't have the strength to even think right now, let alone quiz her father more. She had got what she wanted; he had put her mind at ease. She couldn't believe she had even considered that man, that stranger might be telling the truth. She never should have doubted her father. She felt safe again. By now hopefully the police were on their way to her house to get him. When Jasmine finally got home Tim would be gone and everything could return to normal, couldn't it?

The way these thoughts circled in her mind made her feel uneasy, though. It was as if she were trying to convince herself, but an alarm was going off in the back of her mind that she was trying to ignore.

She had never told her father that Tim's girlfriend had disappeared in Belize.

Chapter Forty-Seven

'Listen to me,' Jasmine whispered to Felicity. 'I need you to go upstairs and pack some stuff.'

'What are you talking about?'

'Just grab some money, ID, toiletries and clothes, that sort of thing. Get some bits for your mum, too. We all have to get out of here. Please, please, please just trust me.'

'You aren't making any sense, Jazz. Are you worried about Tim? The police will deal with him.'

'I'll be up in a minute. Please, Flick, I'll tell you everything in a bit.'

She heard Felicity thumping up to her bedroom and the sound of her floorboards creaking overhead as she followed Jasmine's instructions. That was when Jasmine realised that was all she could hear. Her father was no longer speaking on the phone. Where was he?

Jasmine stepped into the hallway, but he wasn't there. The kitchen door was closed, and Jasmine had never seen it closed before. She moved slowly towards it, listening. There were some strange shuffling noises and the sound of metal clanging against the floor, a spoon falling off the counter top maybe.

Jasmine wrapped her fingers around the handle and pressed down, releasing the catch. She held her breath and pushed forward.

Inside the kitchen, her father was standing behind Felicity's mother with his arm locked around her neck, pulling back as she clawed desperately, a barely audible rasp coming from her throat as she saw Jasmine, pleading with her eyes for her to help, to stop him.

'What are you doing?' Jasmine screamed, frozen on the spot. Her father was focused on his task, his left hand gripping his right wrist and pulling it towards him, crushing Felicity's mother's wind-pipe. He didn't even look up, a focus in his eyes that Jasmine had never seen before.

'You never said anything about Belize, did you?' he said, still straining.

'How did you know?' she said, tears brimming over before she had a chance to stop them.

340

'I remember Rosa. As soon as you said her name I thought of that summer. Finding her, getting her to trust me, until eventually she got into the car with me. When she begged for her life, she said she had a boyfriend. They all say that though, so I just assumed she was making it up like the rest of them,' he said, releasing Felicity's mother, who fell to the ground, unflinching as she smacked her head against the leg of the table.

'How could you do this?' Jasmine sobbed.

'It's not something I planned, it's just how I turned out. I never talk about my past but I had a very strange childhood. My mother died when I was young so I was raised by my dad, and he had no business raising children. I saw things that no one should see.'

'Is that a reason to kill people? You could have got help,' she said, unsure why she was trying to reason with him; the deeds were done, the girls were dead.

'There is no help for someone like me,' he said, his face devoid of emotion. 'My dad would take me with him when he went to see prostitutes; he would pick up women in bars, and I would be in the room when he did whatever he did. Your mother and I worked hard to make sure you had a stable childhood with loving parents. I didn't want you to turn out wrong, like I did.'

'So why didn't you stop? All those women. How could you do that?'

'I don't know how to explain it to you. It's something I need to do to survive.'

'Why those girls?' Jasmine asked. 'Is that the only reason we went abroad? Was it all just a front for your sick and twisted shit?'

'Your mother wanted to travel and help people, and I saw it as a perfect opportunity to do what I needed to do. One girl went missing in each place, a place where lots of pretty young women go missing every year. No one suspected me. I realised after the first few times how easy it was.'

'You're talking about it like it's a hobby. You're so messed up.' Jasmine could feel her breath shortening as the tears sprang from her eyes. She wondered if he had ever considered hurting her, or if he ever thought about her when he was hurting those other girls.

'It's a compulsion.' Frank shrugged. 'The only way to stop myself from hurting more people was by allowing myself that one thing every year.'

'Not a "thing", Dad, a woman, a *girl*, not much older than me. How would you feel if someone did that to me?'

'I'm not saying I'm right, I'm just saying this is how I am.'

A thought occurred to Jasmine that she could

barely entertain. 'What about Mum? Does she know?'

'Your mother has nothing to do with this. If you were to tell her . . .' He left the threat unspoken but Jasmine could see the fear on his face. For the first time he seemed to be displaying some actual emotion. So he did genuinely care about her mum. Then how could he do this to her? Oh God, her poor mother. Finding this out would destroy her.

'I'll get help, Jasmine, just don't do anything stupid.'

'You're going to go and tell the police everything you did. Or I will.'

'No. Your mother would go to prison, too. They won't believe that she had nothing to do with it. You think the attention you got when that teacher kissed you was bad? Try having a serial killer for a father. They won't leave you alone, not ever. But if you stay quiet, I'll stop, I'll get help.'

'What about Tim? He won't go away until you pay for what you did,' she said, stalling, trying to keep him busy to distract him from realising that Felicity was still in the house.

'I called him just now. All he wants is money. I transferred our savings into his bank account. He's going to leave us alone. Everyone has a price, especially someone like Tim.'

Jasmine found it hard to believe that all Tim wanted was money. She heard footsteps on the stairs. Felicity was coming down. Jasmine looked at the knife block, wondering if she had enough time to get to one, wondering if she had enough courage to use it. She couldn't let him hurt Felicity.

'Flick,' Jasmine muttered.

'Keep her out of the kitchen. Keep her out or I'll have no choice!' Frank hissed and Jasmine knew what he meant.

Jasmine left the kitchen and grabbed Felicity just as she reached the bottom of the stairs, making sure she couldn't go in the kitchen. She didn't want Felicity to see her mother like that; she might well be dead.

'Are you going to tell me what's going on?' she asked, trying to shake Jasmine off.

'I will. But we need to get in the car.'

What would she tell Felicity? And what should Jasmine tell her mother? Could she really lie to her about this? There was too much for her to deal with. She just had to get through the next few moments, then she would worry about the moments that followed. Jasmine and Felicity rushed past the kitchen door and outside to her dad's car. He must have seen them. They didn't have much time.

Jasmine got into the driver's seat. To her relief,

the keys were still in the ignition, where her dad often left them.

'What are you doing?' Felicity asked, bewildered.

'I don't know, just get in.'

Felicity jumped into the passenger seat and Jasmine started the car, grateful that her mother had insisted on getting an automatic.

Jasmine put the car into drive and slammed her foot down on the accelerator. Felicity continued to ask her questions, but Jasmine couldn't think. It felt as if the worst had already happened, but there was no way that this day was going to end without more death. Jasmine heard and felt a thud against the side of the car.

'Oh my God!' Felicity shouted. 'Stop the car! I think you hit the dog.'

'I can't stop. We've got to go!' Jasmine shouted back.

As she pulled out of the driveway Felicity grabbed hold of the wheel, trying to wrestle control from Jasmine.

'You're not making any sense. What the hell are we doing? What aren't you telling me?'

'We can talk about this later. We just need to get as far away as possible.'

With a quick, forceful tug Felicity pulled the steering wheel so hard that it propelled the car into the wall at the end of the drive. Jolting them both forwards. Unable to move, Jasmine shifted the gear stick so that the car could reverse, but Felicity was now getting hysterical in the seat next to her.

'Will you just listen to me?' Jasmine snapped. 'We have got to go. Now.'

'Not until you tell me what's going on!'

Jasmine looked back at the house. The front door was wide open. Panic set in. Had she just hit her father? She thought of him lying on the ground under the car and was ashamed at the relief that swept over her. Her car door was jammed against the wall, so she couldn't open it enough to get out. At that moment the back door of the car opened on Felicity's side and Frank got in. She was too late.

'Jasmine, you have just made this a whole lot harder than it had to be.'

He deftly whipped his belt over Felicity's head and pulled her back, quickly fastening the buckle and tightening it so that Felicity was struggling to breathe.

'Dad, please!' Jasmine said between sobs. Calling him that felt strange given what he was doing, and what she had just seen him do inside the house. She wanted to appeal to his better nature but she didn't think he had one. He didn't care about her, he didn't care about anyone. Everything he did was self-preservation, so he could carry on with his sick proclivities.

Felicity's breathing was short and erratic, when she could catch a breath. She clawed at her throat and Jasmine thought of Carol doing that very same thing, and now she was lying on the kitchen floor, possibly dead. Felicity grabbed frantically at the back of the seat, trying to find the buckle to release herself. Frank yanked on it whenever she got close. Jasmine thought she could almost see a smile on his face.

'Turn the engine off and come with me,' he instructed Jasmine. 'I need you to help me.'

'There is no way I am helping you,' she spat.

'Fine, then give me the car keys or I finish your friend off here and now. I don't trust you.'

Jasmine looked at Felicity, her black eyeliner streaming down her face as she lethargically tugged at the leather strap around her neck. She slowly handed over the car keys. Her father got out of the car and ran towards the house. She could see he wasn't moving as fast as he would have before the surgery he'd had before the summer. He was favouring his left side a little. She reached over to Felicity and loosened the belt two notches before Frank got back. At least she would have a little room to breathe.

She looked around to see if there was any way out of this, just as the windows behind them started to glow. She realised her father had started a fire. It had taken hold of the living room before he'd even returned.

He got back in the car and gave the keys to Jasmine. She started the car and reversed away from the wall, the metal screeching as it scraped along the brickwork.

'Where to?'

'Just drive, I'll tell you where to go.'

Jasmine drove the car and with her father's instructions they left the town. The roads were empty anyway; there was no one to report her erratic driving. Her dad had let her drive around the big supermarket car park when it was empty, so this wasn't her first time driving this car.

He told her when to stop the car. Felicity was passed out in the passenger seat. Frank unbuckled the belt from around her neck and she slumped forward.

'Where are we?' Jasmine asked, looking around. All she could see was dark green under the moonlight. Frank got out of the car and dragged Felicity out. He struggled to lift her but she offered no resistance. Jasmine couldn't be sure if she was even still alive. How was this happening?

'If I let her live, then it's all over for us,' Frank

told her. 'I'll go to prison and your mother will most likely get taken away, too. You're over sixteen so you wouldn't go into care. You would just be on your own. Are you ready for that? To just be completely alone?'

'It's already over,' Jasmine whispered. 'I can't bury this. She's my best friend! How do you think I could ever forgive you for any of this?'

'After this I'll stop. I promise I will never hurt anyone again,' he said, his mouth saying one thing, but his eyes saying something different.

She desperately wanted to believe him. 'I don't think you're even capable of telling the truth.'

Frank moved towards the cliff's edge as quickly as he could, clearly in pain now as he carried Felicity, desperate to put her down, his stagger uneven and laborious, the physical exertion taking its toll. He wasn't supposed to be moving around this way, the doctors had told him to take it easy. Jasmine rushed forwards as she realised what he was about to do. But she was too late.

She watched in horror as Frank tossed Felicity over the side, as though she were nothing. Jasmine reached the edge just in time to see Felicity's body tumble into the sea.

Chapter Forty-Eight

Now

The lights inside the house are off but when I press down on the handle of the back door, it creaks open. The house smells musty; the kitchen is half missing, doors gone from cupboards, blown floorboards and smears of dirt on the walls. The years have not been kind to this house; decay and abandonment seep from every crack in the walls. I feel responsible for this, too. If I had stayed then maybe it would have been different. I know I would have been different.

Coming inside has released me from the choke-hold of the past. Was this all I needed to do? Did I just need to be here? To face it head on? A circle has been completed by me returning to this place, the ghosts of my past all in one place ready to be dispatched. I hear a noise, the sound of a chair scraping against floorboards.

'Who's there?' a voice comes from upstairs.

I brace myself. They can't hurt me anymore.

'Jasmine? Is that you?' The voice calls out my name. My secret is out. I am discovered.

'Yes,' I say reluctantly. 'I'm home.'

Chapter Forty-Nine

Then

Before she had time to think or even feel anything, her father's hands were on her shoulders.

'Please, Jasmine. You need to forget this ever happened. Otherwise people will find out; your mother will find out, and then I can't be held responsible for what I'll have to do to keep my family together.'

Was he genuinely expecting her to agree to this? What would he do if she said no? Would he push her? The certainty with which she had defended him to Tim was gone now, and that Jasmine was gone now, too. Whatever happened, there was no going back to the life she'd had before. She just had to decide how many lies she could live with.

'OK,' she said, her voice breaking. 'You win. Let's go home.'

Her father pulled her into an embrace, squashing her arms by her sides like he used to do when she was little. He kissed her on her wet cheek.

'I love you,' he said, looking into her eyes. Where Jasmine had once seen love, now she could see nothing but relief and maybe even a little excitement. He had lived to kill another day. She hugged him back, the comforting embrace of her father, a million memories coming flooding back of hugs like this between them, as far back as she could recall. He was always her comfort, strong and dependable, logical but funny too. She realised now, in these last few moments, that the man she remembered was never real; he was the mask her father had used to cover the monster.

She squeezeed him tightly one final time before twisting and pushing him as hard as she could. Her father stumbled backwards, unable to control his footing, clutching at his side and looking at her with a mixture of fear and surprise. She closed her eyes when he ran out of ground and went over the edge, the sound of his cry getting further away as he got closer to the sea, until it stopped and there was silence.

354

Jasmine was alone.

She looked back at the car pulled over on the verge. She had to go home. How could she face her mother after everything that had happened tonight? How could she tell her what she had done; what Frank had done? Jasmine took a couple of steps before the weight of the last hour hit her and she fell to the ground, all energy and adrenaline gone. She just wanted to lie here for ever. Sobbing, she finally clambered to her feet and made it to the car, the cliff's edge firmly in her rear-view mirror as she drove away.

Chapter Fifty

Now

The house that I have feared for so long is whispering to me. This is the first time I have been inside it since that night.

I didn't have the courage to tell my mother what had happened on the cliff, or what Tim had discovered about my father. I had parked the car on the drive and looked through the window at my mother leaning over the sink, a concerned look on her face. She looked so vulnerable and I just couldn't face her and tell her what I had done. She was alone, waiting for my father to come home, waiting for me to come home. But we never did.

My guilt about what happened that summer is too much for me to bear. I have suppressed it for years but now, looking at the front door, I can feel it as strongly as I did back then.

I hear the sound of stairs creaking and even the footsteps sound familiar, as though everyone comes down the stairs in their own way and this way was my mother's.

'Jasmine?' she says, as she is standing in front of me, blinking back tears. I can tell she wants to hug me, but I don't want that. She looks behind me to check I am alone.

'Hello, Mother,' I reply, balking at the sound of my own name. A name I haven't used for more than half of my life.

'I didn't know if I would ever see you again.'

'Well, here I am.' It comes out more harshly than I'd intended. I'm not as happy to see her as I should be. Just being here makes me feel sixteen again, makes me feel like that girl who was told lie upon lie upon lie. The girl I had to bury, and the friend I never got to.

'Look at you. Look at your hair,' she says, reaching forward to touch it. I pull back before she can. I hadn't realised before now how angry I would be with her. I can feel my heart thumping, and what I mistook for fear as I approached my old home has now shown itself as rage. I wish this house didn't exist anymore. I look at my mother and wish there was nothing left of my old life. Nothing. She looks old. She is wearing clothes that I remember, faded and tatty but still quintessentially her. Her hair is grey and unkempt. Her skin has lost that glow it used to have and now looks off-colour in some way. It's like everything stopped when I left, like my mother stopped living. I want to feel guilt, but I can't. A part of me is glad that she has suffered, still angry at her for marrying my father, for making me a part of this awful family.

'Did you send me the note?' I ask.

She nods. 'By pure luck I saw you when I was out shopping one morning in town. I didn't know how to approach you after all of this time had passed and so I went to the hotel and gave them a note to pass on to you. I had hoped you might come and see me sooner.'

'Why did you want to see me?'

'I'm not well, Jasmine,' she tells me, her eyes filling with tears. 'The doctor said I need a new liver.'

Something about the way she speaks to me seems false. I don't believe her story about just spotting me in town; I look completely different in my Felicity disguise. The years apart have made me more objective, I don't look at anyone with the same naive filter that I used to. I have my parents to thank for that.

'Well, you can't have mine.' Again, I sound harder than I'd meant to. She's just an elderly woman who has lost everything – but somehow I don't forgive her. 'I came back to find out what happened to the missing girl, to Mandy Green. When I saw that news report I thought maybe Tim was back – or Dad.'

'What happened on that day?' my mother says.

I'm not an easy person to manipulate anymore. It's like I can see the machinations, I am always looking for them. It was one of the things that drew me to Chris: his lack of ulterior motive. These past sixteen years I have felt so guilty for what I did but now, back here, I look at my mother's forlorn face and I can't help feeling it's just a mask.

'First, tell me what happened to Tim,' I say, looking for a reaction. 'Why do you have his car?'

'Your father called me when you were at Felicity's house that night. He told me that you and that Tim had a relationship, that he had been *with* you right under our noses, grooming you. I was beside myself; after what happened with your teacher how could we let it happen again? We offered Tim money to leave you alone. A lot of money. He didn't need that car anymore.' She started sobbing.

I pause, looking at my mother. She looks so lost, so sad. But I know better.

'You're lying, I see it now. Why have you been following me?' I say.

She flinches and takes a step back.

'All this time I thought you were the innocent bystander, the ignorant wife. But then they found Tim's body in the woods and I knew that you had a bigger part in this than Dad ever told me. How did he get there?'

I see my mother considering her options. She seems confused and trying to work out how to play this. She has aged so much in the last sixteen years, a shadow of her former self. I see the exact moment she decides to give me more information as it crosses her face, as if there is still some way out of this for her that might win me back.

'I made a deal with Tim. He told me his suspicions about your father, showed me the photographs. I told him if he came to the woods with me and dug a grave, I would kill your father and Tim would have his revenge. I told him that you had confided in me. I told him I was scared of what Frank was going to do. I wasn't wrong to be scared. You have no idea what your father was capable of.'

'But Tim ended up in a grave not far from Hannah Torrence. There is only one person who could have put him there.'

My words throw her a little; she isn't understanding my logic. I realise in that moment that she
thought maybe I hadn't run away alone on that
day, that maybe my father had taken me and we
had gone together, leaving her alone in this house.

'Jasmine, what did you do? What happened to
your father?' she says, her hand moving to her
mouth as she catches her breath. Was this ever
about seeing me again, or was it about seeing him?

'I had no choice. He killed my friend.'

'He told me to deal with Tim and then he would
come and get me when you had calmed down,
that he needed to make sure you weren't going
to do anything stupid. You would go away for a
couple of weeks until you had come to terms with
everything. I thought you were both coming back
for me, but you didn't. He never came back for
me,' she said, sinking to the ground, sobbing.

'If Hannah Torrence was there, that means you
killed her, too.'

'I don't expect you to understand. Your father
had certain . . . needs. It was my duty as his
wife to make sure they were fulfilled. I was
driving back from my book group and I saw
Hannah walking up the road. I could see she
was around your age and so I pulled over and
asked her if she wanted a lift. Told her I was
your mum.'

'Christ, you used my name?' I say, wondering how I never noticed what kind of people they were. Wondering if that kind of behaviour was hereditary.

'I didn't plan it, the opportunity just arose. And your father had been so down. I just did it on the spur of the moment. It was such a gift when you later told us about that creep of a teacher accosting you at the fair. There was a way to give the police a suspect.'

'You killed Morrell too, I suppose?' I say, looking down on her sitting on the floor. So pathetic, but I have no sympathy at all.

'He caught your father hiding the girl's wallet in his car, so your father had no choice but to get rid of him.'

'But you buried Hannah in the woods?'

'I got her body from the shed, where it was hidden. I wrapped her up in blankets weighted with stones from the garden and plastic sheeting around her, so Tim wouldn't notice she was a bit smaller than Frank. I told Tim it was your father, that I had killed him as promised. Tim put her in the boot of his car himself. I followed him up to the woods. When he threw her into the grave I waited for him to cover her up and then as he was walking back to the car I hit him over the head with the spade. I buried him nearby.'

'When?'

'After you and Frank didn't come home that night. Tim kept asking where Frank was, why you weren't back yet. He was a mess. He sat me down and told me what he had told you, told me to call the police, said he was scared that Frank had hurt you. As if your father was capable of that,' she scoffed.

'I played the role of worried mother perfectly. I told him you were staying with your friend to be safe and that he should lie low until I had spoken to Frank. He believed every word of it, because it was what he wanted to believe.'

'Why? What could possibly make you and Dad do those awful things? Did you know about the girls he killed from the start?'

'First, tell me what happened the night you left,' she insists, holding onto the console table to pull herself to her feet. She's struggling but I make no effort to help her.

'I told Felicity, as you know. Dad worked out that we knew and he killed Carol, Flick's mother. Then he took me and Flick to one of the clifftops. He threw her over the side and wanted me to just let it all go so we could carry on the way we had been. But how could I? I had no choice but to stop him.'

'You killed him?' Lisa spat. 'How could you?

364

He was your father. He loved you so much. You meant the world to him.'

'How could I? How could *you*? How could you let him kill all of those young women? They didn't deserve that.'

'When you're in love with someone, you love every part of them. When I met your father he changed my life. You don't understand what it was like for us, growing up the way we did. Your father's childhood was chaotic. My family life was horrible. When we met it was like everything made sense suddenly,' my mother explains.

I wonder if she even knows what love is.

'You never told me how you both met.'

'Your father worked at one of those travelling fairs. He came by my hometown a couple of years in a row and we fell for each other. When he moved on from Harlow, I decided to follow him. Then one night I caught him with one of the girls and I flew into a rage. He belonged to me. So, I hit her, hard, so many times. I choked her, almost killed her. Poor girl had to go into hospital. Your father said it was the first time in his life that he had ever felt special, or important. His dad was a really bad man,' she says, as if Frank wasn't, 'and he had always felt completely isolated.'

'So watching you beat a woman half to death turned him on, is that what you're saying?' You read about people like this but it never quite makes sense, how they can find each other, how the violence starts, how they first realise that this is the life they want.

'It was like we understood each other,' she said, as if reminiscing about happier times. 'We tried a few times to recreate that moment, but it's difficult here. Even when you pay the girls there's always a risk that they won't like the violence that comes with it.'

'All these years I thought you didn't know. But then they found Tim's body and I worked out that you were the only person who could have done it. So all that time you were a part of it, too? Dad admitted that was why he wanted to travel every summer, but he said you had no part in it. Was he lying?'

'Yes, that's why we travelled. There are some places where it's much easier to get away with hurting people than others. We weren't the only ones doing it, I'm sure.'

'But you didn't just hurt them, did you?'

'At first, yes – but then it went a bit further. The first time the girl died was honestly an accident. We just got caught up in the moment. I didn't mean to kill anyone.' My mother says this as though she is looking for sympathy, as though there is even the slightest chance that I can forgive her.

'Oh God.'

'After I fell pregnant we had to think of a way to keep doing what we were doing, but keep you safe as well. So we joined the charity; it was a perfect cover. We had everything we could possibly want. Opportunity everywhere and no real scrutiny of what we were doing. A lot of the times these charity projects are largely invisible to the authorities.'

'You have to go to the police. You have to give yourself up,' I say, knowing she won't.

'I'm not going to do that.' She dismisses the idea as if it's of no importance. 'I just wanted to see you one last time. I don't have long left and I thought it was important to say goodbye,' she tells me, the look on her face warm and loving. I know it's a lie though. It's no wonder I don't trust people.

'Why Mandy Green? Did you know she was Mr Morrell's daughter?'

'I felt it had some kind of poetic nostalgia to it. I was trying to get you to come here but I didn't know where you were. I assumed the news reports would mention her father, but I guess I gave them too much credit. I didn't think things would unfold the way they have; I didn't think they would unravel completely. I wanted to talk to you and this seemed like the best way to do it. Doesn't it feel like we have unfinished business?'

I can tell that she is itching to embrace me, she wants me to tell her I forgive her and that it will all be all right, that I will stay if she wants me to. She wants me to tell her that I still love her, and I can't.

'I didn't even know if it would work when I took her. I was driving past the bus stop and saw her standing there. It was raining and she looked miserable. You can always tell when someone is ready to give up; it's a gift your father and I both had, I think. She had that look on her face. I offered her a lift and she took it. I gave her a drink with a little something in it and she passed out before she had any time to process what was going on. It was almost too easy.'

'Where is she? Is she dead?' I ask.

I remember the photographs of the girls that I saw all those years ago; they had been subjected to all manner of unspeakable things over a period of time. There was a chance she had kept Mandy alive, especially if she thought my father was coming back with me; some kind of twisted welcome-home present.

'That doesn't matter. Only family matters now, darling.'

'I'm not your family and I'm not your darling. You're a stranger to me. I didn't come here for you, I came here for me. Do you have any idea what it's been like for me? Knowing that I came from this . . . evil? It was bad enough when I thought it was just him. Was my whole life a complete lie? I felt so guilty for what happened to Dad, for taking him away from you, despite what he was. But now I realise I should have killed you too.'

'Do you relive that moment over and over again? Do you savour it?' she asks, a glint in her eye. She misses it.

'No! I'm not like you,' I say. As my mother's words hit me I realise I did the right thing and the guilt I have felt over killing my father all those years ago disappears. If anything, I wish I had seen what kind of person my mother was and dealt with her too. Maybe then Mandy Green wouldn't be missing. I wonder how many more girls would have died if my father and mother had been allowed to continue. I wonder if I ever would have found out, if it wasn't for Tim coming into our lives and exposing them. I feel bad for the things they are saying about him in the papers; he wasn't who they said he was.

'Then we must have done something right. Look at you. You're more beautiful than I imagined you would grow up to be.'

'Where is Mandy?' I ask again. 'Is she here?'

'You call yourself Felicity now?' she asks,

ignoring me. 'She was a good friend to you, it's a shame what happened to her. I know it's hard losing someone you care about.' There's an edge to her voice. I know she is thinking about my father again.

'I didn't lose her, I watched Dad kill her.'

'You changed your hair to look like hers,' she observes. 'You always did look a lot alike.'

'I couldn't be me anymore. I didn't want you to find me. I didn't want anyone to know where I came from. I thought when Dad's body turned up that he would get found out and I couldn't bear the thought of anyone knowing I was associated with him in any way. But it never did turn up, did it? I sometimes wondered if maybe he survived and managed to get away. Start again with someone else,' I say, and for the first time my mother's mask slips, her face distorted with anger, not an expression I have ever associated with her. I have hit a nerve.

'Don't be ridiculous. If your father were alive he would have come back to me.'

'You can't know that. Maybe he had it planned that way all along; after all, he's the one who took me up to the clifftop. Maybe you didn't know him as well as you thought you did.' I don't believe he survived but I'm taunting her, to punish her for what she never paid for. Her entitlement is staggering; the belief that they could do whatever they wanted and that was OK because they were in love makes me seethe. I've also realised that every time I mention the girl who went missing, she tries to change the subject. Mandy must be alive still. She may even be here.

I push past my mother. She moves aside surprisingly easily; I can feel her frailty as she stumbles out of my way.

'Where are you going?'

'To the guest house in the garden,' I say. I walk through the kitchen, grabbing the key from the drawer on my way – nothing has changed, only become worn and more broken as time has passed. Everything is dark and dirty, as though she stopped living the night I ran away. I try the handle and look back to my mother. She is struggling to regain her composure. I can see she is weighing up what to do, whether or not she could take me down before I got the door open. I see her decide she can't and so she resumes a weaker stance, as if she is some frail old lady, though she isn't that old. I don't know if her act is for my benefit or if she is preparing herself for when the police arrive.

I walk through the garden and place my hand on the handle of the guest house door. The last time I did this my whole world turned upside

371

down. Was it about to happen again? Nothing could be worse than the things I had already seen, the things I had done. I steel myself and unlock the door to the guest house, taking the key with me so she can't lock the door behind me. I know she is capable of great evil; I don't want to assume that just because I am her daughter I would be spared.

The dust catches in the back of my throat as I enter. It's pitch-black as the windows are all covered, so I run my hand along the wall until I find the light switch. I hear my mother's tentative steps behind me and it crosses my mind that she could swing for me. I'm not convinced about the level of her fragility. On the floor in the bedroom is a mattress and a bundle of what appears to be blankets and an old sleeping bag. It's the same sleeping bag I had seen resting on the chair all those years ago.

'Mandy? Is that you?'

I hear a groan and a pale white arm emerges from under the grey woolly heap on the ground. I crouch and pull the blanket back. It's her; she looks like her mother, like her father, too. Her lips are cracked and she blinks several times to adjust to the light.

'Who are you?' she whispers.

'I've come to help you,' I say, holding my hand

out. A wave of emotion sweeps over me as I think about Rosa, and Felicity, and all those other girls I couldn't help.

Her fingers are cold. I untie her wrists; she is unsteady but she hasn't been hurt physically, from what I can see. I have no idea what my mother planned to do with her, or what she was thinking at all. I wonder how involved my mother was in all the awful things that happened to the girls before they died. I help her stand and we move towards the exit together. When we get to the front door my mother is standing there. I help Mandy rest against the wall and stand in front of her, my arm around her in case my mother tries to do anything stupid. I have no idea who she is, I never did. She is clearly capable of anything.

'What are you going to do now? Call the police?'

'I am.'

She lunges forward, quicker than I imagined she could move. She has a knife in her hand and she swipes it towards Mandy and me. As off-guard as she has caught me, I still manage to rush forward and knock her to the ground, where she lies, her initial burst of energy short-lived.

'They will find out what you did,' she says with a hint of venom in her voice.

'Fine. Tell them what you have to tell them. I'm sick of running.'

I pull my phone out of my pocket and dial the police. I can't live the rest of my life inside this awful lie. I know it will be terrible for Chris and the children if the truth comes out, but the alternative is to be this person for the rest of my days. I can't do that.

'Jasmine, please, don't do this. I don't have long left. I promise I won't tell them anything about you, just let me go,' she pleads, but her eyes are still dead. Her selfishness is even deeper than I thought it was.

'Not my problem,' I say as I hear the ring on the other end of the line. I'm really doing it. I wasn't sure if I would.

My mother clutches at my ankle but I feel no sympathy for her at all; my sympathy goes to her victims.

I hear the voice prompt on the phone 'Police please . . . yes . . . the missing girl from Sidmouth . . . Mandy Green, yes . . . I found her.'

Chapter Fifty-One

When I get out of the interview room, I see Chris sitting on the cold plastic seat in the hallway. He stands up and rushes towards me with his arms outstretched and before I know it they are wrapped around me. I start to cry because I didn't think I would have this again; I didn't think I could. I thought by accepting my past and confronting it I would be destroying everything I have.

'I missed you,' Chris says. 'What happened?'

'I found the girl who went missing. I was the only one who could. I have a lot to tell you, if you want to hear it,' I say, knowing that once I tell him the truth he may leave me.

A police officer steps out of a doorway and walks over to us.

'Thank you very much for speaking to us today. Miss Green's family are over the moon to get her back. Her mother wants to give you a reward.'

'Oh no, that won't be necessary,' I say. If anything, I should be giving Liz Green financial restitution. If I can, when all this is over, I will try to make amends for all the pain my family caused her.

'We'll be needing to speak to you again about everything that happened and go over your statement. We're interviewing the lady who owns the house you found her in. She doesn't seem quite with it. Did she say anything much to you?'

'Not much, no,' I say. Knowing my mother has kept quiet about our connection makes me feel a little better. It may not stay hidden for ever, but for now I am just glad to get the chance to tell Chris on my own terms. Whatever happens after that is out of my hands.

'We'll be in touch,' he tells me, handing me a card. I have already told them how to reach me – that is, if Chris lets me come back home with him. The police officer leaves and we are alone.

'Where are the kids?' I ask my husband.

'Back at the hotel. I booked us a suite; you can move your stuff over later if you want. They're watching movies on the laptop, so we can go for a drink if you want?'

'Let's go for a drive and talk in the car. I think we should be alone.'

We get in the car and he starts driving, I watch the air freshener swinging from the rear-view mirror and the small picture frame with an old picture of Daisy and Lloyd in it.

I start to tell him my story, from the beginning, from the moment Tim came into our lives to the moment I got away, only to meet Chris a few weeks later. It was as if fate had sent him to me, to save me, to save the life that was growing inside me. My little Daisy, who looks more like me than her father – but every so often I see it in the way she walks, the way she smiles and bares her teeth. Those volatile blue eyes that change colour with the weather, with her mood. Just because I now know her father is dead doesn't mean it will be any easier for Chris to hear about who he was.

We drive up to one of the scenic coastal sites, overlooking the green fields that drop off into the sea, and when Chris reaches across to my seat and takes my hand I know it's all going to be OK. We will get through this, together.

Acknowledgements

As I wrote this story I was reminded of my teenage antics in Sidmouth with my best friend at the time. We lost touch when we left school over twenty-five years ago. Midway through writing this book she contacted me after seeing my face on social media. She is also a published writer and I feel so grateful to be reunited with someone who was such a huge part of my life. Love you x

As always, thank you to the brilliant team at Avon Books, especially my editor Tilda, who has been so patient.

Secondly, thank you to everyone at Northbank Talent, particularly Hannah and Diane. It's great to know you guys have my back.

Introvert hugs to all my crime writing friends. I don't know what I would do without you.

Shout out to all the members of the online Facebook crime fiction group CRIME SUSPECT, your enthusiasm for the genre is very motivating!

Special thank you to all book bloggers, readers and reviewers. Your continued support means a great deal. I still read all my reviews and really appreciate everyone who takes the time to write one.

Thank you to my husband and my amazing children. You all mean the world to me.

Thanks to my sister Anna, my Auntie Marie and my cousin Jason for reading all my books.

Thank you to anyone I have missed, I know there are loads.

If you loved *The Heatwave*, don't miss Katerina Diamond's bestselling crime series featuring Adrian Miles and Imogen Grey

Book 1

'All hail the new Queen of Crime' *Heat*

The
Secret

Everything
you *think* you
know is a lie...

KATERINA DIAMOND
SUNDAY TIMES BESTSELLER

Book 2

'All hail the new Queen of Crime' *Heat*

The
Angel

Some things can't be forgiven...

THE *SUNDAY TIMES* BESTSELLER
KATERINA DIAMOND

Book 3

You make it. You break it.

The
Promise

KATERINA DIAMOND

THE *SUNDAY TIMES* BESTSELLER

Book 4

Truth or Die

NOT FOR THE FAINT-HEARTED!

Sometimes the past
comes back to kill you...

Katerina Diamond

Book 5

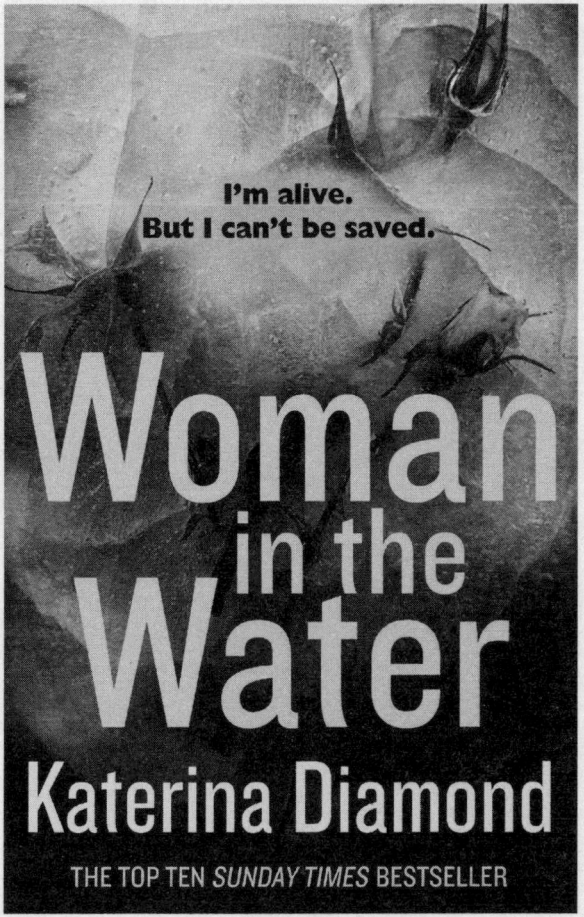

I'm alive.
But I can't be saved.

Woman
in the
Water

Katerina Diamond

THE TOP TEN *SUNDAY TIMES* BESTSELLER

Book 6